LUX ROSE

BORN TO KILL

CYN ALEXANDER

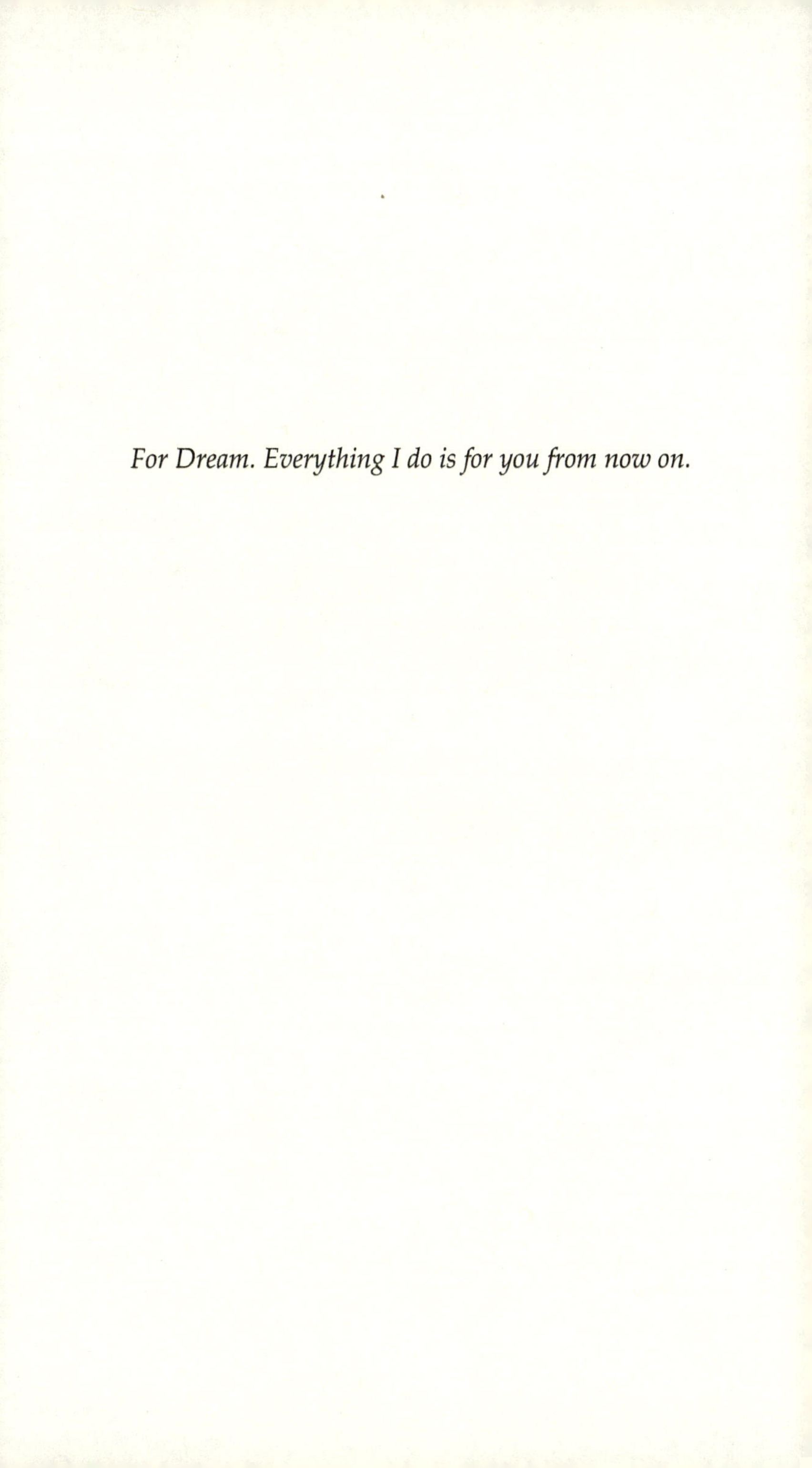

For Dream. Everything I do is for you from now on.

CONTENTS

ACKNOWLEDGMENTS

Thank you so much to my readers! I can't believe I wrote this book in 10 days! I have never done anything like this before, but it is because of you and your excitement of the Anything for the Family series that pushed me to do this.
Don't worry! That series will pick up as soon as Lux is finished telling her story. I promise reading this mini series will help you really appreciate her in the rest of the Anything for the Family series.
I love you all - keep shining!

PROGUE

ow! Pow! Pow!

"You hit the head every single time, nena. Good job," Waylan *said to his nine-year-old daughter as he patted her on the back while simultaneously pulling the target cut out like a body closer to them.*

Lux looked up at her father and beamed before placing the automatic handgun on the table and asking, "What's next?"

Waylan opened his mouth to respond, but Dionne, his wife, entered the soundproof basement and cut him off. "Nothing, baby. Your guests are here, so playtime is over."

Lux didn't know whether to pout or smile. She loved spending time with her father and learning all the cool things he taught her, but she loved spending time with her best friends, too.

"Aw, mami, just one more round?" Waylan begged his wife as he took her in his arms and sprinkled kisses all over her face.

Dionne giggled before swatting him away. "No, Waylan. Besides, I told you not to come down here in your party clothes. I know you two. If you stay down here a second longer, your clothes will be ruined."

She straightened his pink tie before squatting in front of her daughter and smoothing out her pink and frilly party dress. "It's your birthday, Lux. Don't you want to go play and be a normal kid?"

Lux thought about it for a moment. "I don't want to be normal, but I do want to see Mateo and Blanca."

Dionne laughed, and Lux mimicked her mother. She loved her parents dearly, but she hoped when she was older she held as much poise and grace as her mother. She was the definition of class, and she was the best mother. She wanted to be that for her own children one day.

"Come on, then. They're outside, and I saw them eying your gifts. It's time to turn the killer off and become my little princess. Can you do that for me?" Dionne asked.

Lux moved from foot to foot anxiously upon hearing her mother say her friends were eying her gifts. She nodded her head. "Yes, Mama."

Waylan kneeled in front of his daughter next to his wife and looked her in her big brown eyes. "And remember, you can't tell anyone about what we do down here. It's our family secret."

Lux nodded again and then used her pointer finger to make an X over her heart. "Cross my heart."

"But never hope to die," Dionne added.

"Kill instead," Waylan finished, and the family grinned at each other at their little inside joke.

"Okay, mija. Let's get out there before Blanca gets into your presents," Waylan said as he stood up.

Lux sprung into action as she raced up the stairs. No way were her friends going to get at her presents. Not on her watch.

Waylan and Dionne chuckled as they followed the birthday girl up the stairs and through their mansion. Once they got outside, Lux made a beeline for her best friends, Blanca and Mateo, dodging other guests along the way.

By the time she finally made it to them, she had completely transformed into a little lady, tucking her killer instincts away.

"Drop that present, Mateo!" Lux demanded.

Mateo froze at the sound of Lux's voice and turned to face her with a lopsided grin. Blanca looked on guiltily because she convinced Mateo to peek into some of the presents. Before Lux could turn her gaze on her, Blanca slipped into the crowd to find her aunt.

Lux didn't pay her best friend any mind as she gazed at Mateo and his crooked smile. Her heart rate sped up as she took him in. He was wearing a black button up with black slacks and a pink tie that matched her dress perfectly. Knowing their parents, they color coordinated them on purpose.

"Aw, chaparrita. I was just looking," Mateo expressed as he looked at Lux guiltily.

Lux's temper flared. "I told you not to call me chaparrita. I'm taller than you!"

Mateo's lopsided grin was back. "For now."

"Forever," Lux said defiantly.

Mateo walked over to her and slung his arm over her shoulders. "You would marry a man shorter than you?"

Lux thought about it. "No, I guess not."

"Okay, then… chaparrita it is," Mateo replied happily.

Lux rolled her eyes and then poked him in the ribs. "You'd better hope you grow then because I meant what I said. I'm not marrying a man shorter than me."

Mateo smoothed down his tie nonchalantly. "Mama says you have to marry me no matter what."

Lux didn't respond because her parents told her the same thing, but it was okay with her. She'd been conditioned to love Mateo since they were old enough to walk. Their families had been planning their wedding for years now, and when Lux turned twenty-five, she was going to marry the only boy she ever loved. It was like a fairytale, and Lux couldn't wait until the day arrived.

CHAPTER 1

16 Years Later

"This shit wasn't supposed to happen, man," Mateo said as he blinked back tears and pinched the bridge of his nose while looking down at the twin caskets in front of him.

Lux walked up beside him and placed a hand at his back while her long thick mane blew in the wind. Mateo barely registered that she was there as he fought his tears. His parents... the only family he had, were laid up in matching golden caskets ready to be buried six feet under.

The most Lux could do was empathize with him. She truly couldn't comprehend what Mateo was feeling nor did she ever want to find out. Her parents were her everything, and she knew she would feel broken and lost without them. She also knew how much Mateo's parents meant to him. They were a close-knit family, just like she was with hers.

Although they grew up together and were arranged to be married ever since they could remember, Lux had never grown very close to his parents. Not like he had with hers. His parents always treated their union like a business transaction, which it was, but Lux truly loved their son and hoped after they married they would start seeing her more as a daughter-in-law and not a business partner. Now, they wouldn't have that chance. The fire that burned their home down ensured that. Lux thanked whatever higher being there was above that Mateo had been staying the night with her when it happened.

Finally, Mateo turned to face her. He ran his large hand down his face and straightened up. He was in public, and he wasn't trying to look weak. Lux saw the shift in him, and she understood. While she had been groomed to kill, Mateo had been groomed for the streets. He and his family ran the largest drug cartel in Cuba, and rule number one was to never show weakness in the public eye. Lux understood that notion. It was the same when she was on a job.

Showing weakness was a sure way to get caught up, and that was never an option.

"Let's go," Mateo said, looking down into Lux's cocoa brown colored eyes. Luckily for him, when he hit puberty at around fourteen, he grew several inches, finally deeming him taller than Lux. He wasn't the tallest man around, but he was definitely taller than her by several inches, finally earning the right to call her chaparrita, which meant shorty.

Lux's thick but perfectly arched brows pinched together as she looked up at him through her shaded glasses. "You don't want to stay for the burial?"

Mateo shook his head. "I can't see that, mami. I've made my peace with the fact that they are gone. It's time to ride out so we can start making moves." He pulled her close to him and placed a kiss on her forehead. "Plus, we have a wedding to plan."

Lux smiled nervously at that, but she didn't comment further. She simply pulled away from her fiancé and grabbed his hand. He squeezed her small hand in his, the same one with the heavy diamond on her ring finger, and led the way through the crowd. Nobody said anything to him because he had that *don't fuckin' talk to me* look on his face. He was feared enough in this country for people to give him a wide berth wherever he went. Even if they felt compelled to give him their condolences, they didn't.

They made it past the crowd of people and to the edge of the cemetery when Blanca spotted them as she was speaking with her aunt.

"Mat! Lux!" she called, waving them over.

Lux smiled at her best friend and tugged on Mateo's hand. "Blanca, what are you doing way back here, chica?"

Blanca smiled bashfully, tucking a strand of her sleek jet black hair behind her ear, which did nothing because her hair was cut into a short bob, so it just flopped back into her face.

"You know I hate funerals," Blanca replied, and Lux nodded. She did know this of her best friend, but she assumed Blanca would suck it up to be there for Mateo. They were considered The Three Musketeers growing up and even now into adulthood. They'd been best friends since diapers, and Lux would have thought she would have gotten past her issues with funerals to be there for her best friend, but she had to constantly remind herself that not everyone was built like her. Her best friend definitely wasn't. Not even close. She was as shy and innocent as they came. Lux feared nothing, but Blanca feared a lot. They were complete opposites, and that was why they clicked so hard.

"It's all good, B," Mateo said, almost distractedly as he leaned over and hugged Blanca. Blanca hugged him back tightly, but Lux could tell Mateo really just wanted to get out of there, so she turned to address Blanca's aunt so they could be on their way.

"Ms. Dalia, how are you?"

Dalia smiled up at Lux and patted her cheek. "I am well, nena. How are you holding up?"

Lux smiled down at the older woman. She was the sweetest woman, and it was no wonder Blanca turned out the way she did. Blanca was truly an around the way girl. Her parents abandoned her when she was a baby, leaving her with her mother's sister, Dalia. Dalia took Blanca in and raised her, providing for her as best as she could, but they were still not very well off. Not even a mother, Dalia took on the role of a single mother who was struggling to make ends meet. Still, she raised Blanca to be hard-working and as sweet as they came.

Mateo and Lux used to practically live at the beach when they were little. At three years old, they made friends with Blanca. Soon, Dalia and their parents made acquaintances, and from there, Blanca became a permanent fixture. She didn't have the same upbringing and lifestyle as Lux and Mateo, but she fit into their group like she belonged, and it was because she did.

Lux glanced at Mateo, who was talking softly with Blanca, before focusing in on Dalia again. "I'm just trying to be strong for Mat."

Dalia smiled up at the young woman, her soft brown eyes crinkling at the corners. Dalia was a whole head shorter than Lux, who was five feet eight inches. She had jet black hair that was always braided in one thick braid down her back, and her hands showed hard work and labor.

"You don't always have to be the strong one, Lux. Since you were a little girl, you were such a force. It is okay to let others be strong for you sometimes," Dalia advised.

Lux smiled warmly at the woman and took her hands. "I know, Ms. Dalia. Now just isn't the time. I know if I ever need Mateo to be strong for me, he will be. But now is my time to be strong for him."

Dalia looked up at Lux and struggled with what to say next. Finally, she settled on, "It's also okay to lean on people other than Mat. I love that boy, but he isn't the end all be all, Lux. Remember that. For as long as

I can remember, you two have been so wrapped up in each other… I just want you to know you have other people that love you."

Lux nodded with a smile. Dalia had always been concerned about how intense Lux and Mateo's relationship was. She had no idea it was arranged. Blanca was sworn to secrecy. To the rest of the world, they were lifelong lovers finally getting married. Hell, that was how Lux saw it, too. Because she truly did love Mateo. However, due to recent events and some nervousness of her own… she made the decision to postpone the wedding. She felt Mateo needed time to grieve, and she needed time to come to terms that this shit was finally happening. She was really about to be Mrs. Mateo Rodriguez. The issue was, nobody else knew she had come to this decision. She planned to talk to Mateo and her parents that night at dinner.

"I hear you," Lux finally said before turning to Mateo. "You ready to go? I'll shoot my parents a text and let them know we're out."

"You're leaving?" Blanca asked, confused.

Mateo nodded. "Yeah. I'm ready to get out of here."

Blanca looked up at him with sad eyes. "I understand." She turned to Lux. "I'll find your parents and let them know you went home. See you tomorrow?"

Lux smiled at her friend's expression. Tomorrow was Blanca's birthday, and she promised her a girl's day. "Thank you, B, and of course. I'll text you in the morning."

Blanca smiled sweetly before pulling Lux in for a hug. The two friends squeezed each other, and Lux fought back tears. She wasn't much of a crier, but for some reason, that hug was pulling some emotions out of her. She pulled back and grinned at her friend, blinking the tears away.

"Te Amo," Lux said.

Blanca smiled. "I love you too, Lux."

Lux grabbed Mateo's hand, and together, they left his parent's final resting place, ready to unwind until dinner. Lux was sure it was going to be eventful.

CHAPTER II

othing to it but to do it, Lux. You got this, she thought while she played with the food on her plate. They were sitting in the formal dining room having dinner. The room had a modern day feel with gold accents and black throughout.

Her mother outdid herself with the red beans and rice, fried pork chops, greens, and cornbread. Lux hadn't even tasted it, and she knew it was bound to be good as hell. She loved when her mother made dishes from her home in Atlanta. It was shit they didn't eat on a day-to-day basis in Cuba, but it was food that Lux grew up on because her mother missed her home state, and food was a sure way to feel right back at home.

The issue was, Lux's stomach was in knots, so she didn't have much of an appetite. She wasn't one to get nervous about shit, but when it came to her loved ones, they had the power to cause this foreign feeling. She never wanted to disappoint them, and postponing the wedding was sure to be a huge disappointment. It was something they had been looking forward to and building toward for twenty-five years.

She finally put her fork down and glanced up at Mateo, who was at one end of the table to the right of her, and then at her parents. Her mother was sitting across from her looking at her father, who was at the other end of the table. Dionne was looking at Waylan lovingly as he spoke. Lux smiled. They had always been an inspiration to her. Although their marriage was also arranged, they found true love within each other. Lux wanted that, and as she grew up and formed a bond with Mateo, she knew she was lucky enough to have it.

Arranged marriage was something her family had been a part of for generations. The Rose family would link up with a powerful family in the drug business. The drug business was where the Rose family made their money. The bosses in the game always had a steady need for their services, so they made it happen. By ensuring that the two families were bound together, it ensured longevity in the Rose family business. Lux would have access to Mateo's contacts, just like Waylan, her father, had access to her mother's family contacts. As those contacts got older, the jobs become less, but by that time, another wedding was in place, and the parents could retire while the child carried on the legacy. It had been this way for generations and had worked out perfectly. Lux didn't want to let anyone down, so she knew she had to reiterate that she was absolutely still marrying Mateo. She couldn't imagine not doing so. She just needed a bit more time.

She cleared her throat, and the surrounding conversation ceased.

"What's wrong, baby?" Dionne asked, forever in tune with her daughter's moods. Dionne was the nurturing parent, raising Lux like a normal parent would. She was emotionally there for her child, she made sure she did well in school and went to college, she taught her how to cook and clean and take care of herself, and she loved on her fiercely. Waylan, on the other hand, was militant with her. As a child, she was woken up at five in the morning every day, no days off. He would train with her in the basement in the mornings until it was time to go to school. When she was home and after schoolwork and dinner, she would head back to the basement and train some more with her father.

By the time she was five, she knew how to shoot small handguns, load them, take the apart and reassemble them, and clean them. It was how Waylan was raised, and he was parenting the only way he knew how. Lux loved it, though. She was truly a daddy's girl. Waylan loved his daughter, too. It wasn't all work and no play. They just got a kick out of playing differently. They would play games with guns, seeing who could make the most head shots on the practice dummy, or they would see who could stab a dummy more times in one minute. As she grew older, they bonded over hand to hand combat, how to properly throw grenades, and how to make homemade bombs in a pinch. Call them crazy, but they had a blast, and Lux soaked up every single piece of information he threw at her. She looked up to her parents, just in different ways.

"Nothing, Mama," Lux finally responded before she looked at Mateo and grasped his hand. She noticed that his plate was hardly touched, too, and her heart broke for him. She knew he was hurting if he wasn't eating. That man loved to eat, normally. It only gave her more ammunition to say what she needed to say. Looking into Mateo's eyes, she said, "Papi, I know we are meant to marry next month, but I really think we should postpone it a few months. Maybe until the end of the year? You need to properly grieve, and I don't want this to be too much for—"

"No," Mateo and her father said at the same time, completely cutting off her speech.

Lux knew they would be against it, but she needed to be heard. No was not an option. She needed more time, and even though Mateo didn't realize it, so did he.

She ignored her father and looked at Mateo. "Baby, it's only a few months. I don't want our day to be clouded by sadness. I've been looking forward to this since we were old enough to understand what a wedding was... please, baby. I just want things to be perfect."

She gave him sad eyes, and they weren't even fake. She wasn't lying about what she just said. She did want the day to be perfect and not clouded by sadness on his behalf. She also wanted to be clear about her own feelings. She wanted to get rid of this nervousness and shock that this day was finally coming. She didn't want to spend the day in a daze that she was finally marrying the love of her life. Something in her just felt *scared*. It was a feeing she wasn't used to, so she needed time to shut that shit down.

Mateo had always given Lux her heart's every desire. It didn't take much for him to look at her and feel his resolve melting. Waylan could sense it. Lux always had that power over the poor boy, so before Mateo could give in, he spoke up. "Lux, no. We have had this date planned for three years. This is nonnegotiable."

Lux finally looked at her father and said, "I spoke with the wedding planner. She said she could make the change and is just waiting on me to confirm. It is negotiable, Papa."

"No," Waylan said simply.

Dionne looked like she was going to intervene, but Lux's temper already flared, so it was too late. She threw her napkin down on the table and looked at her father angrily. "I'm sorry, Papa. I didn't realize you were the one getting married." She pressed her hands into the table and leaned into them. "Let's get one thing straight… I am still marrying Mateo. I love him, Papa. I just think with everything that has happened, our focus has shifted, and we need to make sure your future son-in-law is okay. I know you lack real human emotions, but I thought you might at least try to understand this."

Without waiting for a response, she spun on her heels and stalked out of the room. She made her way through the mansion, not slowing until she got up to the third level of the house and into her room, her place of solace. It was decorated in shades of blue with pops of orange. Her room reminded her of a sunset with the colors. Her king sized bed was calling her, but the balcony facing the ocean was calling her even more. Her room was her solace, but the ocean was her place of peace. She stepped out onto the balcony and took a deep breath, breathing in the salty air. It was nighttime, but the lights from her house lit up the area just enough for her to make out the dark ocean lapping against the shore. She briefly wondered if she should go down there, but she decided against it. It had been a long ass day, and she would be bound to fall asleep listening to the waves if she went to the beach.

A few moments later, she felt a presence behind her. Lux never got snuck up on. She learned long ago how to be so in tune with her surroundings that she knew when she was not alone. Without looking, she asked, "Did Papa send you?"

Mateo chuckled. He never understood how she was able to do that, know he was there without even looking. He stepped behind her and said, "No, mi amor. I excused myself and came to find you."

Lux sighed before facing him. "I love you, Mateo. I'm just worried about you."

"Shh.. mami. It's okay. I don't like this shit, but let's talk about it tomorrow, eh? It's been a long day."

Lux relaxed into him and kissed his neck before pulling back. "You're right."

"You sure you want to marry me still?" Mateo asked nonchalantly, but Lux could see the uncertainty in his eyes. She hoped he wasn't questioning her love for him.

"One day very soon, I will be Mrs. Rodriguez," Lux said, smiling up at him.

Mateo's face melted into a smile, his pink lips spreading, and his thick brows un-knitting. "I like the sound of that, but I'm just hoping we will make it that far. Your padre looked pissed when I looked like I was even thinking about giving into you."

Lux looked worried. Her father being angry with Mateo could be a dangerous thing. She and her father had identical dangerous tempers. Mateo noticed her uneasiness, and he laughed. "Relax, chaparrita. It isn't like he is going to kill me."

Lux laughed nervously with him. Another thing about the arranged marriages her family partook in… the other family thought they were in the drug business until after the weddings. It was safer that way. Once they were legally bound not to say anything about their spouse being assassins… they were safe to tell them, which meant for now, Lux had been keeping her true identity a secret from Mateo.

Mateo threw his arm around her and pulled her close. He kissed her nose, and she smiled. She always felt happy in his arms. He knew how to pull smiles out of her unlike anyone else. He placed a kiss on her lips, and their tongues instantly found each other. As soon as Lux could feel his dick hardening, she pulled away and grabbed his hand. "Come on. Let's get ready for bed."

Mateo had been living with her family since the fire. Once they were married, they would move into their own home, but for now, house hunting was not at the top of their list of things to do. He had his own room at the Rose mansion, but he always stayed in Lux's room.

He groaned, knowing exactly what *get ready for bed* meant. He and Lux had yet to have sex. Get ready for bed meant exactly that. Lux was a proud virgin. Knowing the man she was going to marry her entire life really shaped her sexual appetite. She had this fairytale-like dream about how their wedding and honeymoon would look, and when she had her mind set on something, she followed through with it. Unfortunately, that meant through Mateo's entire life, he had to follow along and get with the Lux Rose program.

"I hate when you pull away, mami. I wasn't going to do anything—"

"Ah ah ah, Mateo Rodriguez. Don't do that. You know the rules. Now, are you going to come cuddle with me until we fall asleep or what?" Lux asked, turning to face him once they were back in her room with her hand on her hip.

Mateo sighed. "Yes, but let me take a cold shower first."

Lux rolled her eyes. "So dramatic."

He chuckled before pecking her lips and going into the grand bathroom that was attached to her room. Lux changed out of the black clothes she had been wearing all day and into a silk Vera Wang nightie. She climbed into bed, her body sinking into it comfortably.

Before Mateo even started his shower, Lux was drifting off into a peaceful sleep.

CHAPTER

III

The next morning, the first thing Lux did when she woke up was grasp her phone from the nightstand closest to her. She saw that it was nearing ten in the morning, which meant she had slept for damn near fourteen hours, which wasn't typical for her. She must have been dead ass tired for her body to have claimed that much sleep.

"Shit," she muttered as she wiped sleep crust out of her eyes.

She glanced over her shoulder and noticed Mateo was gone, probably awake and attending some kind of business, even though she tried insisting that he take some time off to deal with the aftermath of his parents passing. He had to deal with the insurance claim on their home, figure out their life insurance policies, and some more shit, but to Mateo, the most important thing was ensuring he could find and reach out to all their connects. He knew most of them, but all that information and shit went up in flames with his parents. The only saving grace he had was a safe deposit box at their bank, and the fact that he had a hefty bank account on his own. His workers provided useful for helping him navigate shit, so he was doing alright on his own, but he had big shoes to fill after his father's passing, so he was stressing himself out trying to do that shit. He knew he would get all the money his parents had in their accounts once he settled the insurance policy, but he wasn't worried about that at the moment. He was worried about making sure he could keep making hundreds of thousands of dollars.

Lux shook her head as she sent Mateo a text asking where he was. She got out of bed to get ready for her day, the bathroom her first stop. A day with Blanca was exactly what she needed, and what better way to spend her best friend's birthday than to shop and eat until they couldn't anymore? Manzana de Gomez was just the place to meet all their needs for the day, and Lux knew Blanca was going to be excited as hell to learn that was where they were going. Everything would be on her, and no wasn't in her vocabulary when it came to Blanca today. She knew her friend couldn't afford the things at the luxurious mall, but Lux could, and she always had a giving heart.

Once she was finished showering, she walked back into her room with a towel wrapped around her and made her way to the opposite wall where the door for her closet was. She stepped inside, and the sensor light turned on, illuminating all her clothes, shoes, accessories, and purses. She smiled. She may have been bred to be an assassin, but she was just as girly as they came. Her mother made sure of that. They bonded over shopping and trips to the nail salon. Her mother made sure her room was equipped with a closet space big enough to house all the items they got on their many shopping sprees, and Lux knew she was blessed.

She decided to go with something simple, so she went to the section with her jeans and selected a dark washed pair before going to where her bodysuits hung and selecting a cream-colored tank top one. She slipped the bodysuit on, not needing a bra because she was lucky enough to have big breasts that sat up without needing the support. Wiggling into her fitted skinny jeans was a tougher task since her curves were outrageous. Her thick thighs gave way to wide hips and a big ass, but finally, she was able to zip and button the pants around her slim waist before walking over to the floor to wall mirror on the far side of the room. She grabbed the brush that sat on the shelf and brushed out her long and thick black hair. She didn't really have curls like her mother, but her hair wasn't as silky and fine as her father's, either. She was somewhere right in the middle, having her mother's thick texture and her father's silky waves.

Once her hair was tangle-free, she pulled it up into a high ponytail, not caring that it was messy because she knew it was going to be hot as hell that day, and if she tried laying down her edges, they would only sweat out.

Finally, she swiped some mascara on, put some lip gloss on, picked out a cream colored Prada purse, and slipped on her cream red bottoms. She strutted back into her room and rummaged through the purse she had been using yesterday, grabbing her wallet, keys, and sunglasses and placing them into her Prada bag before leaving her room.

Her heels clicked against the expensive heated marble floors as she made her way through her home. She smiled up at the high ceilings and large paintings gracing the walls. The home she had been raised in was massive but homey. It was comfortable and filled with things, so it felt lived in, but it wasn't cluttered.

When she became a teenager, her parents renovated the third floor, which was the top floor of the home, and turned it into her part of the house. There had been days where she wouldn't even have to see her parents because she had everything she needed up there, complete with a kitchenette and her own TV room.

Finally, she made her way to the second floor where her parent's room was as well as their offices, before she reached the final set of stairs that would lead her to the main part of the house, the first floor.

By the time she made it into the kitchen where her mother was cleaning up breakfast, Lux was contemplating if she should change shoes because her feet were already hurting. She decided to thug it out before greeting her mother cautiously. After last night, she wasn't sure how her parents were feeling about her, and she was relieved that her father wasn't around.

"Hi, Mama," Lux said before kissing her mother's cheek and sitting at the island while she watched her mother move around the kitchen. This big ass house was maintained by the queen that lived there and always had been. Because of their line of work, Lux learned from a very young age that hiring employees to do shit for them was just not in the cards. In return, each of them had to be exceptionally clean and know how to take care of themselves. They spent at least one day a week cleaning together and going grocery shopping for the following week in her childhood. They all kind of did their own thing now, but back then, it was a family tradition that was upheld religiously. Honestly, Lux couldn't see it any other day. On weeks that were extremely busy, she looked forward to chore day with her parents as a kid and even a teen. It was where all their bonding moments as a unit came from. Some of her fondest memories were on chore day.

"Hey, baby." Her mother eyed her knowingly with a smirk on her face. "How did you sleep?"

Lux gave her mother a small smile before grabbing a piece of papaya out of a bowl with assorted cut up fruit and popping it into her mouth. She had never been the biggest fan of breakfast, but she could eat fruit all day, every day. She chewed on the sweet fruit for a moment before saying, "Good, actually."

"I'm sure you did." Dionne chuckled. "You and your father always sleep your best after confrontation. Nothing like me, I swear."

Lux giggled. It was true. She and her mother were nothing alike personalty-wise, but in the looks department, they were practically twins. Her mother had smooth dark skin, tightly coiled black hair that reached her shoulders, and thick perfectly arched brows. Their bodies were damn near identical, too. Wide hips, big asses, and huge breasts. Lux was her mother's twin, but she was a few shades lighter with mocha colored skin, and her hair was long and thick.

"How is Daddy?" Lux asked. She wasn't nervous about her mother's response, she just genuinely hoped it wasn't some bullshit.

Her mother wiped her hands on a kitchen towel and rolled her eyes. "Chile, you know that man is stubborn, just like you."

Lux nodded. When her and her father did have a disagreement, it would go on for days because neither of them would budge on their stance. It normally took her mother coming in and playing mediator to get the issue resolved. Lux and Waylan were entirely too much alike, which meant they bumped heads every now and again. Dionne could tell this situation would get out of hand if she didn't nip it in the bud, though.

"Mama, am I wrong for not wanting to get married right after Mat's parent's died?" Lux asked, looking for a genuine answer.

Her mother arched a brow before coming around the counter and sitting next to Lux. "Is that why you're trying to postpone, Lux?"

Lux rolled her eyes. Her mother knew her too well. She sighed and replied, "Mama, it's all just coming up so fast. It's like I suddenly turned twenty-five, and things started happening. I know I had all my life to think about it and look forward to it, and I still am looking forward to it, but I am nervous. And with his parents passing… I just want everything to be perfect. I don't want my nerves or his sadness to cloud our day."

Dionne patiently listened her daughter until she was finished before she smoothed Lux's baby hair's back and said, "I was nervous too, you know?"

Lux scrunched her face up. "To marry Papa?"

Dionne nodded. "Chile, yes. At the end of the day, getting married is always a good reason to have anxiety. Throw in the fact that it's an arranged marriage… let's just say I understand the nerves, baby."

Lux nodded in relief and tried not to smile. She loved when her mother's southern twang came out. Growing up in Cuba, but having a mother who was a US citizen, it meant she had dual citizenship, but she never exercised that right. It was always important that she lived in Cuba to keep away from where she worked. It was always how her family operated. Live in Cuba, kill in the United States. When her parents got married, her mother had to give up her life in Georgia. They still visited often, but not as much as they used to.

"How did you get over those nerves?" Lux asked.

Dionne shook her head. "I didn't, baby. They lasted all the way up until my eyes met his at the altar when I was walking down the aisle. All that other bullshit melted away when I laid eyes on him."

Lux smiled. "So, you think I shouldn't postpone?"

Dionne chose her next words carefully. "Lux, I have always been an advocate for you making your own decisions. You know I never wanted you to start killing, and I damn sure didn't want you to have to go through an arranged marriage. Hell, I didn't even know your father killed for a living until after we married."

"Would you have married him still?" Lux asked. She had to admit, she was a bit nervous about how Mateo might feel about her real job. It was different for a woman being an assassin and her husband finding out. Would he feel less like a man or some shit? Would her forbid her to kill? Not that Lux would listen… but still. These were questions that ran through her mind often. Mateo's mother had been a stay at home mom and wife, and there were many times he hinted he would want Lux to work less and be at home more once they got married. She loved Mateo, but killing was in her blood. It was something she had to do, and she feared he wouldn't understand that.

Dionne smiled. "I would have, but I would have set some ground rules."

"Like what?" Lux asked.

"Like I wouldn't have allowed him to get you into the family business. I never wanted any of this for you, but when you became old enough, and Waylan started teaching you about weapons, I saw the way your eyes lit up. That killing shit is in your blood. Something I'll never understand."

"But you've killed before, Mama," Lux pointed out.

Dionne nodded. "Only when I had to, though. My family made sure I could defend myself if need be, but growing up in the streets, the princess of a drug lord, and how your father grew up, were two different things."

Lux nodded. "I understand. Why do you think he is so hell bent on this date? What is the rush? It isn't like Mateo's parents are around anymore, so there technically isn't a contract to uphold."

"Baby, you know your papa is a man of tradition. This is the only way he knows. I think he is worried that if he gives you time to think on it, you might pull out of the plan. A plan that has been in place for twenty-five years."

"I love Mateo, though," Lux replied, confused by her father's logic.

Dionne laughed. "Your father doesn't think like that, Lux. You know he's militant. If we have a plan, he is going to want to stick to it."

"I am sticking to it, though. I just want to push it back a little," Lux argued.

Dionne looked at her daughter for a moment before saying, "I'll talk to your father, okay? He will come around. As long as Mateo is good with it, then I don't see any harm in holding off on the wedding for a few months."

Lux smiled in relief. "Thanks, Mama. Mat and I talked a bit last night. I don't think he is really fond of this idea, either, but I will try to get him to see my view on things. Where did he sneak off to, anyway? I know he stopped down for some breakfast."

Dionne laughed. "You know he did. He didn't eat last night, so I knew he would be hungry this morning. I know his parent's deaths are taking a toll on him but no way is he going to be skipping out on too many meals." The two laughed before Dionne said, "He just said he had some business to handle."

Lux nodded just before her phone chimed. She thought it would be Mateo, but when she fished her phone out of her purse and glanced at the screen, she saw it was a text from Blanca letting her know she was ready to go. "I have to go, Mama. Blanca is waiting on me."

Dionne nodded. "Tell her happy birthday. Her gift should be delivered by the time you two get home."

Lux hopped up and smiled, knowing Blanca was going to freak at the present her parents got her. "I will, Mama."

She waved and slipped out of the kitchen with a lot on her mind but feeling better about the decision she made.

"Hey, chica," Blanca said as soon as she got into Lux's Maybach.

Lux leaned over and hugged her best friend. "Happy birthday!"

Blanca giggled and hugged Lux back. "Gracias."

"De nada," Lux replied before pulling away and checking her phone that sat in its holder on the dash. Mateo had yet to respond to her text from earlier, but she knew he was probably busy, and it wasn't out of the ordinary for them to go hours without communicating.

She put her car in reverse and pulled out of the short driveway leading to Blanca's house. They never spent much time over there, despite Mateo and Lux urging Blanca to allow them to do so. They loved Dalia, and they loved her cooking even more, but Blanca was always insistent that they spend time at

Mateo or Lux's houses because they were bigger with more to do in them and in nicer neighborhoods. Blanca grew up in what would be considered the hood in Cuba. They called it the slums, but Lux was never scared to go over there, and Dalia kept a neat and cozy home, so she never saw the issue.

"What's the plan for today?" Blanca asked after she put her seatbelt on and Lux put the car in drive.

Lux glanced over at her friend and asked, "You up for a little shopping?"

The smiled fell from Blanca's face. "Pay day isn't until—"

"Girl, when have I ever been pressed over money? Plus, it's your birthday. Everything is on me today," Lux assured.

Blanca wrung her hands in her lap. "Are you sure?"

"Positive," Lux replied with a grin. "And Mama told me to tell you she has a gift being delivered. It should be there by the time we are finished."

Blanca giggled nervously. "I hope it isn't another car."

Lux laughed loudly. On Blanca's sixteenth birthday, her parents bought her a car after consulting with

Dalia first. Blanca proudly still drove that thing, too. She took good care of it and was proud to have her own set of wheels, even if it was almost ten years old now. What Blanca didn't know was that she was right. Her parents had bought her a new car because they were so impressed with how well she took care of the old one. They figured Dalia could drive Blanca's current car, and she could have the new one.

"You never know with them. You know they love you like a second daughter," Lux replied vaguely.

"I know," Blanca responded timidly.

The two fell into a comfortable chatter during the rest of the drive, and when Lux pulled up at Manzana de Gomez Luxury mall, Blanca's brown eyes went wide. "Lux, this is too much! You know it's all high-end stores!"

"Duh," Lux replied as she found a parking spot. "Nothing but the best for you."

They got out of the car, and Lux linked her arm through Blanca's and asked, "Where should we start?"

Blanca looked down at the Gucci slides Lux got her last year for her birthday and then shyly glanced up at her friend. "I really like these slides. Maybe Gucci?"

Lux's smile broadened. "Couldn't have thought of a better place to start myself."

Several hours later, after many stores and a lunch where they ordered every appetizer on the menu, Lux and Blanca were getting ice cream cones before they left the mall. Lux's feet were killing her, but at least they made the smart decision to make frequent trips to her car so her arms weren't hurting, too.

An observer by habit, Lux noticed Blanca had been checking her phone frequently and smiling. Matter of fact, she had been known to do that for as long as Lux could remember. Blanca was a very private person, even with Lux, so Lux never pushed too hard, but today, she felt like being nosy.

"Who you texting?" Lux asked, trying to peek over Blanca's shoulder.

Blanca shooed her friend away and smiled before licking her ice cream while they walked over to a nearby bench to watch the sunset while they ate their cones, the mall still bustling with activity behind them. "None ya."

Lux giggled. "Uh uh. Tell me something. Hell, I don't even know if you're still a virgin. You know all about me and Mat… no fair."

Lux put on her best pout, and Blanca laughed. "That's because you are both my best friends, and I have grown up with you two. It's different. I have no choice but to know all about you two"

Blanca rolled her eyes, and Lux shrugged. "Still… You know you can trust me, right?"

Blanca thought about it before saying, "I know. Okay, there is a guy I've been dating for a while now—"

"How long?" Lux asked, a grin stretching across her face before she licked her ice cream to stop it from melting in the heat.

"Honestly? A long time," Blanca replied with a giggle.

Lux's eyes grew wide. "You sneak! Spill all the tea. Is it someone I know?"

Blanca's brows rose, and she shook her head sharply. "No. But we have had sex."

Lux was in her zone. She lived for girl talk just as much as she lived to watch a mothafucka bleed. "Is sex as great as people make it seem?"

Blanca smiled timidly, looking down at her ice cream. "It's better."

"Oh, my God," Lux replied, but before she could ask any more questions, her phone chimed in her purse, and just like that, she turned from the around the way girl into the killer. The chime came from her work phone. Only certain people had access to that number, and any time it made noise, it meant there was money to be made.

She pulled the phone out of her purse. It was identical to her normal phone, so Blanca would have never known the difference, but Lux did. The text simply read the name of the target, the city, and gave a timeframe for when the shit should be done followed by three more words. *Make it Messy.* A moment later, her phone buzzed again, and she saw a wire came through to her account with seventy-five thousand dollars. They would send another twenty-five thousand at completion.

She put the phone back in her purse and looked at Blanca. "Sorry to cut this little chit chat short, but I have to go. Work stuff."

Blanca nodded. She knew Lux had a part in her families *drug* business, which meant Lux sometimes had to drop everything to work. "It's okay. You've made my birthday another one to remember."

"Anything for you, Blanca," Lux replied, standing and throwing the rest of her cone in a nearby trash-can. Blanca followed suit, and together, they walked back to the car, Lux's killer instinct amping up every step of the way.

CHAPTER  IIII

"**B**itch!" Roy, the man tied to the chair, hollered after Lux cut off his pinky toe.

He was completely naked and bloody as hell. She loved jobs like this. Ones where she could take her time and enjoy her craft. This shit made her pussy wet, and on the private jet home, she was sure she was going to pull out the mini rose that was tucked into her purse and utilize that shit.

"Aw, what's wrong, papi? Not enjoying yourself?" Lux asked as she looked up at him from where she was sitting on the floor in front of him. Six out of ten of his toes were lying on the floor around her. She looked around at them and giggled. "I suppose not, huh?"

There was something about cutting a nigga's toes off that Lux found hilarious. She had ever since she was a young teen and started doing jobs with her father. Fingers were fine and got the job done, but toes were fucking entertaining. Hearing a nigga scream about his *toes* was priceless.

"Just kill me, and get this shit over with," he breathed, and Lux chuckled. They had been at it for hours. She already burned him, beat him, and electrocuted him before she took to fucking around with the knife. She was growing tired, and she knew once those toes started coming off, she was close to her end. That shit was her climax.

She stood to her feet and smiled down at him. "You know, I think you're right. It's about that time. Plus," she looked down at her Cartier watch, "I have to get back home for food tasting for my wedding. Doesn't that sound fun?"

"Fuck you, you fucking psychopath," the man spat, and Lux's brows knitted together.

"Now that wasn't very nice," she said calmly before raising the bloody knife and saying, "I don't know what you did to the nigga, but Bentlee Paxton sends his best."

The man's eyes widened before Lux shoved the knife into his left eyeball. She let it sit there for a moment before forcing it upward and directly into his brain.

The man's screams ceased, and all was finally silent. Lux smiled at her handy work before looking around the room. "The cleanup crew is going to have fun with this shit."

She stepped out of the abandoned warehouse, careful to keep her specialized suit on that covered her entire body. It was a sheer material, so she could easily see, and her victims could see her, but it insured she didn't leave not one ounce of evidence behind.

When she got to her rental, she stripped out of the suit so she wouldn't fuck the car up since it had blood spatter all over it and put it into a plastic bag she had in the passenger's seat. Finally, she got in the car and started it up, briefly checking her phone before putting it in the holder on the dash and dialing her fiancé.

Mateo had been texting her all day trying to make sure she was going to be at their food tasting appointment. She had half a mind to push it back, but there wasn't any point in that since they were still getting married, and this shit had to get done. This appointment had been set for months, and the caterer had flown in from the US to meet with them.

She waited patiently for Mateo to pick up, thinking his shit was about to go to voicemail, when he answered, seeming out of breath. "Hello?"

"What are you doing?" Lux asked as she put her rental in drive and made her way to the Airbnb where her things were. She easily navigated the streets of Detroit since she had been there many times. Driving in the States was always a different experience than driving in Cuba, but her father taught her to do both so she could be self sufficient in every job. Being a loner was not new to her, and she quite liked the peace her job provided. In Cuba, she knew everyone and always had social interaction, but when she was on a job, she was left alone to her thoughts, and it was something she had grown to love.

"Uh, nothing, chaparitta. I was just getting a workout in. Where are you? I been calling and texting all day. Your father said you were handling some business. Are you going to make it to this food tasting in a few hours?" Mateo asked.

Lux looked at the time on the dash of the car and did a quick calculation in her head. If she hurried, she could make it. "Yes, papi. I will be there."

"You sure?" he asked skeptically. "I ain't doing this shit by myself, Lux. You know I'm not really into all this wedding planning shit."

Lux giggled. "I know, Mat. I got you." She paused for a second before asking. "Papi... How do you feel about postponing the wedding... I mean, really?"

Mateo blew out a breath before responding. "I don't like it. We have been looking forward to the day for a long time, so I'm disappointed, I guess..."

He let his sentence fall off, and Lux's heart constricted a little. "I just think it's for the best, you know? We have so much going on. We can set a new date to look forward to."

Mateo hesitated before responding. "I still don't like it. I know I give you everything your spoiled ass wants... but this is something I am hesitant about. I feel like you don't want to marry me anymore or some shit."

Lux's frown deepened. "Let's talk about it tonight. I will see you in a few hours. Just meet me at the place."

"Lux, don't be late," Mateo warned, dropping the subject.

"I got you, papi." She hung up the phone and put her foot on the gas, knowing she needed to hurry if she wanted to make it on time. She tapped out a quick text to her pilot with one hand on the wheel before focusing back on the streets and thinking about how she was going to get both Mateo and her father on board with her desire to put the wedding off. Everyone acted like she was calling it off altogether, which was frustrating as hell.

After twenty-five minutes of driving, she pulled up to the house she was staying at and quickly went inside, leaving the engine running. She grabbed the plastic bag from the front seat before exiting the car and making her way into the house. She had only been gone from home since yesterday evening, and she arrived in the states late last night. As soon as she touched down, she got a few hours of sleep before hunting Roy's ass down and completing the job. It was a shame she couldn't stay and enjoy the city and the bomb ass house she rented, but that was her life.

Her overnight bag wasn't even unpacked. She quickly made her way through the modern two-bedroom home, making it to the master bedroom. Lux stripped out of her clothes and placed them in the plastic bag and then walked over to the electric fireplace that was in the room. An important rule in booking her Airbnb's... the place had to have a fire-place. Preferably an electric one.

She placed the plastic bag in the fireplace and then flipped the switch to turn it on. She smiled when the flames activated, and the plastic from the bag melted away, leaving only the bloody transparent suit and the clothes she was wearing underneath. Even though the leggings and t-shirt hadn't been exposed to Roy or his blood, she always took that extra step. Another thing she always did that was nonnego-tiable was take a shower after every single hit. It didn't matter if she was a sniper and nowhere near the body or any blood... if she did a hit, she was taking a shower afterward. These were the militant rules her father instilled in her at a young age. When she was a child, after every lesson in the basement with him, he would order her to shower, even though they hadn't killed anyone. Eventually, it became habit, and he no longer had to open his mouth to say anything.

Grabbing her body wash, shampoo, and conditioner from her bag, Lux walked her naked ass into the master bathroom and started the shower, hopping in and making quick work of thoroughly washing her body and then her hair. When she was finished, she dried off, brushed through her hair, washed her face, and then got dressed in the extra pair of leggings and hoodie she packed in her bag.

The fireplace made quick work of her clothes. She checked it as soon as she was finished getting dressed and saw all there was left were ashes. She turned the fireplace off and grabbed her bag, leaving the room and then the house entirely, making sure to lock up.

She slid back into the driver's seat and pulled off, glancing at the clock once again. She smiled. She was right on time. As long as the private jet could take off on time, she knew she would make the food tasting and not have to hear Mateo's mouth.

When she pulled up to the airstrip, she tapped out a text to the group chat she had with her parents, letting them know she was on her way home. She always made sure to do that. It was confirmation that the job was complete and that it went well. Even though Lux was a professional, as her parents, they still worried a job might go wrong one day, especially her mother.

She greeted her trusty pilot, Anthony, and made her way to her seat. Anthony had been working for her family since before she was born. He was an older Black man from New York, and he was the nicest man Lux had ever met. He had three kids and a plethora of grandkids, who he updated her on every time he saw her.

"Did you have a good trip, Ms. Rose?" he asked.

"How many times do I have to tell you to call me Lux?"

Anthony put his hands up in a playful mock surrender with a smile in his eyes. "Sorry, Lux. You know me."

She smiled. "I do, and my trip was fine."

Anthony didn't know what the Rose family was all about nor did he want to. He was just happy with the pay and the flexibility of the job. Granted, he was always on call, but sometimes there were weeks between calls, and he was more than okay with that because each trip paid him well enough to go a year without working if he had to.

"Good. The skies are clear today, so we shouldn't encounter too much turbulence," Anthony said, giving Lux a knowing look.

"Thank God," she breathed.

Anthony chuckled. "Relax. We will be taking off in a few."

Lux nodded and quickly put her seatbelt on before doing a few breathing exercises. She hated flying since she was a baby. It was truly unfortunate that her job required her to fly often, but she trusted Anthony probably more than anyone else in the world because he was the only person she had ever allowed to take control of her life. Everything else Lux did, she did it herself. Even when she was a kid, she preferred riding her bike to get around town than allowing an adult to drive her.

A few minutes later, the plane started to move, and Lux's heart rate sped up. She hated takeoff. Admittedly, landing was her favorite part of flying because she loved the visual of getting closer and closer to the ground where she belonged.

She closed her eyes and tried to focus on all the food she was going to get to eat within a few hours while the plane took off.

CHAPTER

"I'm so full," Lux groaned as she rubbed her bloated stomach before falling back on her plush bed.

Mateo followed her, lying on his back on the bed and staring up at the ceiling. "Shit, me too."

"That's honestly an accomplishment. Hats off to the caterer because my baby likes to eat," Lux replied with a giggle.

She made it to the food tasting appointment just in time, and she was glad she had. The food was fucking phenomenal, and Lux and Mateo had a hard time narrowing down their favorite dishes. They ended up selecting more dishes than needed, but they simply couldn't let some of them go. Thie menu was a good mix of American and Cuban food. The wedding would be small and intimate since neither family really fraternized with outsiders, and most of the people would be Cuban, but Dionne had a couple family members and friends that were going to make the trip from the States, Lux's godparents included, so she made sure she chose some dishes they would like as well.

A smile spread across her face when she thought about her godparents. Reginald and Trinity Reign. She hadn't seen them in a few years. After they had their twin daughters, the youngest of six, they hadn't been to Cuba to visit her. Before the twins, though, they would make it a point to come at least once a year, and if she was ever in Atlanta, they would take her out to lunch before or after a job if she could fit it into her schedule. The thought of seeing them again this year got her excited. They always spoiled her, and they were some of the only genuine family friends she had. Outside of Blanca and Dalia, Reginald and Trinity were it. Trinity and Dionne had been close friends growing up in Atlanta, and since Lux's father didn't keep friends at all, they were the obvious choice as godparents for Lux, and they took that role seriously. She talked to each of them often and even did jobs for Reginald when he needed.

"What are you over there smiling about?" Mateo asked as he eyed his fiancée.

Lux turned her head and looked at him. "I can't wait to see my godparents. You remember them? You met them a few years back."

Mateo nodded. "When are you going to see them? They coming here?"

"For the wedding, I meant," she replied.

"Ah, and wouldn't it be nice if you could see them next month instead of at the end of the year?"

Lux sat up with a sigh. It had been a long ass day, and she knew Mateo wanted to talk about this shit now, but all she really wanted was to curl up with her man and get some rest. She glanced over her shoulder at him and replied, "Mat, can you please just give me your blessing to do this?"

He sat up and looked at her with a frown on his face. "I don't understand why you're pressing this so much. You say you're doing this for me, so I can grieve or whatever, but I'm telling you I'm fine. Our day will be fine. It's going to be shitty either way that my parents won't be there."

His voice cracked on the last half of his sentence, and Lux could see unshed tears in his dark eyes. She reached out and caressed his face. "You know I love you, right?"

"Do you?" he asked.

Lux's hand fell from his face, and her temper flared, but she took a deep breath and counted to five before responding. "How could you ask me that?"

He shrugged. "All of a sudden you are insisting we push off the wedding… it's just not like you, so what's up? You having second thoughts? Is there someone else?"

Lux reared back and looked at him like he lost his damn mind. There was her temper again, but she stamped it down because she could tell Mateo was just emotional. He had been holding it together since his parents died pretty well, but she had been with him during the long nights where he silently cried. He didn't know she knew about that because she laid still and allowed him to get his emotions out, but she held him extra tight on those nights. Mateo was a man's man. He didn't show emotion… ever, so for him to be wildin' right now, Lux knew it was all a part of the grieving process.

"Mateo Rodriguez. The only man for me in this entire world is you, papi. I've loved you since I was old enough to know what that meant. I don't understand why putting the wedding off is so hard for everyone to understand after such a tragedy."

Mateo stood up. "I don't know, mami. Some shit just seems off with you lately. Like today, why couldn't I reach you? Where were you?"

Lux's brows pinched together. "You know I was working—"

"I couldn't reach you for like ten hours, Lux," Mateo pointed out as he paced in front of her.

"Where is all this coming from? You know my job keeps me busy sometimes, Mat. Just like yours does. We have always had that understanding. I don't get mad when you can't pick up the phone for me," Lux pointed out. She was trying hard to keep a level head about this, but the entire conversation was rubbing her the wrong way. Mateo had never complained about her working before, so she wasn't sure where this was coming from. She didn't want him to start asking too many questions because it would lead to ones she simply couldn't answer. It was an oath she had with her family. Outsiders were never to know what her family did. The only person in the world that did outside of her family was Reginald Reign. She wouldn't be surprised if Trinity knew, too. It just wasn't something she discussed with her because she didn't do business with her. Lux knew how to keep that shit completely separate.

The only reason her father and mother trusted Reginald was because they did business with him on a deep and personal level. Not even Mateo or his parents were warranted that kind of trust, and had his parents still been alive when they got married, Mateo would have been sworn to secrecy not to tell them. The penalty was death. Her family did not play about that shit at all. The quickest way to get caught was by allowing too many people in on their secret. Above anything else, the Lux family cherished their freedom. Not even the clients they did business with knew who they were. They never met, they never even talked on the phone. Everything was done through email. They were given the contact information by drug dealers, who got that shit from the family that was married into theirs. The operation was seamless. Reginald was the exception. The only friend they worked with, and the only nigga alive that knew what they were into.

"Which is fucking weird. What kind of woman doesn't get all pissy over that kind of shit?" Mateo spat.

"What kind of bitches have you been dealing with to know that?" Lux snapped, her anger slowly getting the best of her.

Mateo shook his head. "Ain't no bitches, Lux. It's common sense. Like I said, this shit is feeling mad suspicious."

Lux was at a loss for words. Her and Mateo rarely ever argued, and if they did, it was over petty shit. Never had either of them accused the other of cheating. It was honestly unthinkable. They were born to be together, and that was just that.

"Mat—" before she could finish her sentence, her work phone chimed.

Silence stretched between them as Mateo eyed her. "You gon' get that?"

Lux sighed. This was the absolute worst timing. Jobs were so fuckin' unpredictable. Sometimes she went months without getting one, and sometimes she had them back to back for weeks. Normally, her heart would flutter excitedly at the sound of that phone. This shit right here, at this movement, though, pissed her off, but she had never ignored a job. It was bad for business. Plus, she never wanted to ignore money.

She pulled her phone from her hoodie pocket and looked at the screen. *Tory Smith. Chicago. By midnight tomorrow. Quick and clean.*

"Let me see that shit," Mateo snapped, grabbing for the phone.

Lux instinctively slapped his hand away with a mean mug on her face. "No, what the fuck? This is my business phone, you know that. I don't get all up in your shit, don't get up in mine."

Mateo chuckled, but Lux knew there wasn't a damn thing funny.

"Like I said, suspect as hell," Mateo said before turning to leave.

Lux sprung up from her bed and grabbed his arm in a firm grip. "Don't walk away. What the fuck is up with you?"

He turned to her slowly, looking down at her with a deep frown on his face and his thick brows drawn tight. "Nothing, Lux. We ain't gotta get married next month. You got it."

He snatched away from her and walked out of the room. Lux stood there with her phone in her hand looking at the door with her mouth hanging open. She wanted to go after him and beat his ass, but she took several deep breaths. Dishing out pain was not how she was raised to deal with loved ones nor was it ever a thought that crossed her mind before, but

Mateo took her there for a brief moment as visions of her cutting off his ugly ass pinky toe flooded her mind. She didn't to kill him, but for a moment, torturing his ass sounded damn good.

She shook her head once she got her thoughts under control and started the process of packing another go bag while she simultaneously texted Anthony that she had another job. Once he confirmed he would be at the airstrip within an hour, she focused on packing what she would need. She grabbed her laptop and a few devices that helped Lux track people down before going into her closet and grabbing a few pairs of disposable clothes. She made sure she had enough toiletries before walking back into her bedroom. She was exhausted, but she thrived when she didn't sleep, honestly.

Just when she finished packing, her mother entered her room. "Hey, baby."

Lux looked up and gave her mother a half-hearted smile. "Hey, Mama."

"What's going on?" Dionne asked as she moved further into the room and sat on Lux's bed.

"What do you mean?" Lux asked as she busied herself with zipping her bag.

"I mean besides the fact that your face is all scrunched up, Mateo just walked out of here in a fury."

"He left?" Lux asked, surprised. The sun was starting to set, and she wondered where the hell he was going. She figured he was just going to go to the living room or the game room or maybe his room… or hell, the pool, but for him to leave was odd to her. He didn't have any other friends besides Blanca, and Lux knew her friend was working late tonight.

Dionne nodded and asked, "So, what happened?"

"He accused me of cheating, Mama," Lux replied incredulously.

Dionne smiled at her daughter sympathetically. She remembered the days when her and Waylan were engaged and she got frustrated with all the strange calls and days he went MIA. She glanced down at the bag sitting on the bed as Lux sat down next to it with a sigh.

"You got a job?" Dionne asked.

"Yeah, and suddenly he thinks because I'm not easily accessible and want to postpone the wedding that I'm cheating," Lux scoffed. "Maldito idiota."

Dionne chuckled before standing up. "Give him some grace, baby. He's thinking irrationally right now. Talk to him when you get back and smooth things over. You know you love that man."

"Fuck him right now," Lux said as she stood up. She was irritated with how Mateo handled their conversation, and she hated to be accused of some shit she wasn't doing. She was frustrated with the entire thing. If he kept fucking around, she would call off the wedding and really fuck his world up.

She knew she needed to calm down, so really, the job that came through was actually a blessing.

Dionne shook her head. "You don't mean that, but you're a hothead like your father, so I won't try to convince you otherwise. Come on, I'll walk you out."

Lux allowed her mother to loop her arm through hers before she grabbed her bag and allowed her to pull her through the house, secretly seething the entire time.

CHAPTER

A couple days later, Lux was finally caught up on sleep and feeling less angry at the world. Mateo put her in such a sour mood that not even shooting a nigga right between the eyes made her feel better. By the time she got home from that job, all she could manage was to fall into her bed and into a deep sleep.

She finally woke up an entire sixteen hours later dazed and confused. She looked around the room and noticed it was exactly how she left it. Her go-bag was still in the middle of the floor along with her clothes. Mateo wasn't the cleanest man to walk the earth, but he surely would have picked up behind her had he been home. She was typically a light sleeper, so she would have woken if he had come in the room, even if she did fall right back to sleep, but that hadn't happened. Her sleep had been uninterrupted, and that made her frown.

She got out of bed, scratching her head, her fingers getting caught in her wild mane that now needed to be tamed. She was butt ass naked and in desperate need of a toilet and a shower, so she made a beeline for the bathroom and handled her business.

By the time her bladder was relieved and her body was clean, her head was clear enough to piece some shit together. Mateo hadn't been home since their argument. Lux's brows furrowed as she walked into her closet and selected a pair of cutoff jean shorts and a plain purple tank top. She took her time getting dressed and brushing through her hair before grabbing her phone and making her way out of her room and through the house.

She found her parents in the family room, cuddled up and watching TV. They looked up when she entered, and her mother smiled. "There she is. The dead has risen."

"I sure hope not. I put most of them there," Lux joked, and her father barked out a laugh while Dionne rolled her eyes playfully.

Lux's eyes moved to her father, and she smiled timidly at him. "Hi, Papa."

She hadn't seen him since she requested to postpone the wedding, so she wasn't sure how he was feeling about her at the moment. Shit had been hectic since then, and she got the feeling that he had been hiding out from her, but when he smiled back at her, she felt relief wash over her.

"Come here, mija," he said as he held one arm out while patting the couch next to him with his other hand. Lux did as she was told and melted into her father's side while her mother was cuddled up on his other side. "My girls. What more could a man want, eh?"

"To kill," Lux replied seriously. That was her logic. If she didn't have shit else in this world, she knew she had the power, guts, and means to kill and get away with that shit. That was the ultimate blessing in her eyes.

"Uh, true," Waylan agreed after giving his daughter's statement some thought.

"Oh, you two," Dionne said after sucking her teeth.

Lux stared at her mother blankly. There were things about her mom she would never understand. Her lack of passion for killing was one.

"You know I love you, right?" Waylan asked Lux as he hugged her to his side tightly.

Lux's eyes widened. She knew her father loved her. It was just rare for him to actually express it. "I know, Papa."

He nodded. "I know I can be stubborn, Lux, but certain traditions and things have been instilled in me from birth. Much like they have with you. I can get stuck in my ways, but luckily, we have your mama here to keep us both balanced."

Lux chuckled at that because it was true. As much as she loved her father, her life would be completely different if it was just the two of them. She was fully convinced she would have no heart without Dionne Rose.

"Glad you finally realize that," Dionne quipped.

"I always have, mi vida," Waylan expressed before kissing Dionne on the forehead and looking back at Lux. "What I'm saying is I will leave this wedding business to you. It's unfortunate that Benita and Castillo are dead," he said, referring to Mateo's parents, "but their death has technically released you from any obligation to the Rodriguez family. I just implore you to think about your career and your future. We have rapport with Mateo. Marrying him will ensure you will always have clients to send jobs your way—"

"Papa," Lux interrupted what she was sure was going to be a long drawn out speech about the way their family business worked. "I know all this already. I am still marrying Mateo. I just want a bit of time is all. I love Mat. I know love isn't always the first thing you think of when you think of a wedding, but it's a factor for me just as much as my career is. You two have truly balanced me out."

Lux's face fell slightly, and Dionne picked up on it right away. "Have you talked to Mateo, Baby?"

"Talked to Mateo about what?" Waylan asked as he looked between his wife and daughter.

Lux sighed and said, "We got in an argument the other day. He accused me of cheating because I'm not easily reachable at times… you know, when I'm working. It all came from out of nowhere, Papa. Has he even been home in the last few days?"

"I haven't seen him," Dionne replied.

"Neither have I. Call him, Lux. If you really love him, then you should reach out," Waylan reasoned.

Lux huffed, just the thought of it making her angry. He was the one that walked out on her and was rude to her. Why should she be the one to reach out first? She pulled away from her father and said, "I'm going to call Blanca and see if she wants to go to the beach."

Waylan chuckled. "Good. If I can't talk sense into you, I know she will. You know she was just as excited about this wedding as I was."

Lux stood up and then arched her brow as she looked down at her father. "Excited, Papa? You aren't excited. You're looking forward to being relieved that I went through the with tradition."

"Ohhh, burn," Dionne said before cackling.

Waylan looked between the two and then bellowed out a fake laugh. "Very funny."

Lux shrugged. "You know I'm right."

Waylan grabbed a throw pillow and tossed it at Lux. She caught it easily with a giggle. "Want to fight, old man?"

Waylan waved her off. When she was younger, they would spar in hand to hand combat often, but he was getting old, and Lux was sure to beat him. He didn't feel like getting embarrassed today, especially in front of his wife, so he said, "Call Blanca."

Lux giggled. "That's what I thought."

She turned to walk out of the room, and just before she disappeared from sight, Waylan threw another pillow at her. Lux was too quick and aware of her surroundings, though. Her ears were trained to hear the smallest movement. She turned at the last second and effortlessly caught the pillow with a triumphant smile. Waylan laughed while shaking his head, and she tossed the pillow back at him. "Better luck next time, Papa. You know nothing touches me."

With that, she walked out of the room and dialed her best friend.

"So, he just left?" Blanca asked as she eyed Lux from her beach towel that sat next to her.

"Yes, chica. His ass just left and has been MIA since," Lux scoffed.

Blanca nodded. "Have you tried calling him?"

Lux groaned. "Not you too, B."

"What?" Blanca asked incredulously. "How do you know the man isn't dead or something?"

Lux cringed at that. Mateo being dead wasn't even a thought in her mind. She felt bad for the person that ever tried harming anyone she loved. Real bad. But then again, it didn't necessarily have to be murder. He could have gotten into a car accident or…

"Don't do that," Blanca interrupted Lux's tirade of thoughts.

"Do what?" Lux asked as she stretched out on the beach towel and looked out at the waves crashing against the ocean. The sun was starting to set, and Lux briefly cursed herself for sleeping most of the day away, but the way her body was feeling right now, she couldn't even be mad. She was well rested and clear-headed.

"Think the worst. I could see the wheels in your head turning. Just call him," Blanca replied.

Lux looked at her phone from its perch on the beach towel hesitantly. "I don't know, B. I didn't like the way he talked to me, and he honestly hurt my feelings—"

"Then communicate that with him, Lux," Blanca said, almost seeming to get impatient with the conversation.

Lux sighed. "Maybe I will."

Blanca rolled her eyes. "His ass will come crawling back soon, so I don't know why I bothered."

Lux perked up a bit. "You think so?"

Blanca looked at her with a pointed look before adjusting her red bikini top. "I know so."

"How do you figure?" Lux asked, tilting her head to the sun, trying to catch the last few rays before they dipped behind the horizon.

"I been knowing you two most of my life. I know Mateo better than most. He's going to come back," she said. She was so sure of herself, Lux felt she had no choice but to believe her best friend.

"If he doesn't bring his ass back or at least call by tonight, then I'll reach out," Lux decided.

Blanca beamed, and it was the first genuine smile she gave since coming over to the Rose residence. Lux grinned back at her friend before they turned to enjoy the view. After a few moments, Blanca said, "I can't wait to walk down that aisle."

Lux giggled. Since they were little, Blanca spoke about Lux's wedding as if it were her own.

Realizing that Lux never told Blanca about postponing the wedding, she looked at her friend apprehensively to do so. "B, I forgot to tell you…"

"Tell me what?" Blanca replied while keeping her nose turned up the sky, a dreamy look on her face.

"The argument Mateo and I had kind of started because I asked to postpone the wedding."

"And why would you do that?" Blanca asked calmly without looking at her friend, which completely threw Lux for a loop. She was sure Blanca was going to throw a fit.

"Wait, you aren't mad?" Lux asked.

Blanca finally turned to her and asked, "Why would I be?"

Lux eyed her. She idly wondered if Mateo talked to her already and told her about their argument, but before Lux could confirm her suspicions, Blanca sighed and said, "Look, chica. Mateo loves you, and it is no wonder he got upset about you wanting to push the wedding off, but it isn't like you are calling it off all together, right?"

The question hung in the air while Blanca looked into her best friend's eyes waiting for a response. Lux finally nodded her head and said, "Exactly. That's exactly what I've been trying to tell everyone."

Blanca smiled widely before doing a little dance. "As long as I get to wear that fly ass dress still, I'm happy. Speaking of, are we still getting it fitted tomorrow?"

Lux could see the apprehension in Blanca's eyes. She sighed before nodding her head. "It'll need to be fitted either way, B, so yeah. We can go."

Blanca beamed. "I can't wait… but Lux… I do think you need to consider Mateo's feelings in this. Is postponing worth this rift it is causing? Is it worth the money it'll take to push everything back? What about the guests who already had that weekend marked in their calendars?"

Lux thought about it but simply decided to reassure her bestie once again that she would get to stunt on bitches in her bridesmaid dress before the year was up. That was what Blanca wanted to hear… everything else, Lux had to think on. Blanca was making some valid points. Money wasn't a factor. It was understandable why Blanca would think that way, but to Lux, money wasn't an issue. Not to be cocky or anything… she just had a lot of it to spare. Her money was long, and it was hers. Not her parents. She had been working with her father since she was a teen and had a hefty savings account. But Mateo's feelings were something to consider, and she did have to think about her guests... She had a lot to think about, and she did so while Blanca talked her ear off.

The two laid back and enjoyed the cool breeze while they talked about the wedding and the food tasting Lux and Mateo just did. They sat there for hours under the stars talking like they used to do when they were kids before they called it a night. Lux walked Blanca out and then smiled at the brand new Lexus sitting in the driveway.

"I forgot to ask how you liked your new car," Lux said.

Blanca beamed. "Are you kidding me? I love it. I thanked your parents about a dozen times on the phone. I suppose they're sleeping by now, eh?"

Lux looked at her phone and saw it was going on eleven o'clock. "Probably."

"I'll catch them next time," Blanca said before hugging Lux and getting into her car. Lux watched as she drove away before closing the door and making her way back up to her room.

CHAPTER

Her room was dark when she reached it, only the moon shining through the clear balcony door. Still, she could sense someone else was there. Unafraid, she flipped the switch, and her eyes landed on Mateo, who was sitting in the dark with a clear glass of some dark liquor in his hands. Lux wasn't much of a drinker. She liked to keep a clear head. She did like smoking weed from time to time, but even that wasn't often. Being sober was the ultimate state of mind for her.

"You're back," she stated as she moved further into the room. Mateo nodded before taking a swig of his drink. "Why were you sitting in the dark?" Mateo shrugged, and Lux gritted her teeth before asking, "Are you going to speak?"

"What is there to say, Lux?" Mateo finally asked.

"You can start out by telling me where the fuck you been for the past couple of days," Lux snapped.

Mateo stood and marched over to her, his drink still in his hand. "Or you can tell me where you were."

"I was here, what do you mean?" Lux asked in confusion.

Mateo shook his head before taking another drink. "Nah. I mean the so-called job you had to take."

Lux scrunched up her nose at the smell of liquor. "I was in Detroit, Mateo. I had some business to handle there."

"Detroit? I didn't know you had connects in Detroit," Mateo said sarcastically as he looked down at her.

"Now you know," Lux replied, not wavering.

Mateo scoffed and finished off the rest of his drink while Lux sighed and sat on the bed. "Mat, can we please talk? When did we start talking like this to one another?"

"When you decided you didn't want to marry me," Mateo responded matter-of-factly. She didn't understand where his sudden anger had come from. When she initially brought it up to him, he had been patient and understanding. It was like a switch flipped, and it confused Lux.

"Papi, I do want to marry you." She hesitated as she thought about what Blanca told her before taking in a deep breath and saying, "Look, if me postponing the wedding is giving you this much grief, and if it is going to cause us to drift apart… then we can keep the original date."

"You mean it?" Mateo asked before a smile broke out across his face. He looked like a completely different man than the one he was seconds ago, and Lux wondered if that was how she sometimes looked to people. Conniving and deadly one second and as sweet as a teddy bear the next.

"I do," Lux confirmed, and Mateo leaned down and kissed her.

She smiled into the kiss, loving the affection while secretly hoping she made the right choice. He really had hurt her when he talked to her like she was some whore fucking around on him. He should have known better than anyone that she was anything but a hoe. She was saving herself for him, and as their kiss deepened, Lux realized that some of his feelings may have been because he was sexually frustrated.

Maybe he really just needed a little bit of extra attention in that department.

Lux scooted back on the bed, and Mateo followed, never breaking the kiss. She could tell he was drunk because he was fumbling around, trying to get comfortable between her legs. Lux reached down and grabbed for his zipper, and Mateo pulled back, looking down at her with lust in his eyes. "Don't start something you can't finish, chapirrita."

Lux grinned up at him. "You know better than that. You aren't getting any pussy, but I got you."

Mateo smiled, but Lux could see the disappointment behind the smile. It was at that moment that she was glad she decided to call off pushing the wedding back. It was obvious her man needed some pussy, and she was ready to give it to him... just not that night.

"Lay down," Lux said as she tugged at his jeans while he flipped onto his back.

Mateo eyed her as she grabbed the lube from her nightstand and expertly took his dick out of his pants. She lubed his dick up as well as her hands before slowly stroking him with . "Try sucking it, mami."

Lux looked at him and shook her head. "You know I'm saving that for our wedding night, Mat."

Mateo groaned, but it was because her hands were really feeling good to him. His dick was big enough to where she could use both hands and still have plenty of room to play. She had gotten so good at hand jobs since they were teens that Mateo rarely felt like he needed the real thing while she was working her magic on him. When she didn't have her hands on his dick, his curiosity wandered, but while she had him, he was always stuck. She was damn good at what she did, and it only made him wonder how good that pussy and head game were.

He pulled at her bikini top, and one of her large breasts popped out. He pinched it, and Lux moaned. Her purple bikini bottoms were flooded, and she knew Mateo was not going to disappoint. He used his other hand to find her clit, first rubbing it through the soft fabric of the swimsuit. Eventually, he moved the bikini to the side and massaged her clit with his finger. He knew the rules... he couldn't put his fingers inside her, but he damn sure could rub an orgasm out of her.

Lux wound her hips and moaned while she stroked Mateo's thick dick in her hands. The two were like a well-oiled machine as they worked one another over.

At some point, Mateo took her top off completely so he could see her naked upper half in all its glory. Her big titties somehow defied gravity and sat up just right. He imagined his dick working its way in between them, and that was all the visual he needed.

"I'm about to bust," Mateo breathed.

"Me too, papi," Lux shrieked as she felt an orgasm building up from her core.

Mateo's hot cum released all over Lux's breasts, and her juices spilled all over his fingers and onto the sheets. Lux was breathing heavily and fought the urge to lean over on Mateo's chest.

He chuckled at her sleepy face and moved out of the bed. "Let me grab you a towel."

Lux nodded and waited patiently. He came back with a wet towel for her chest and a dry towel for her pussy so she could wipe up all those sweet ass juices. He licked the remanents of her from his fingers while she cleaned up. He had yet to dive face first into her pussy because that was yet another thing Lux wanted to save for marriage. Tonight's activities were as far as she was willing to go, so he was happy she the wedding was back on track. He was ready to feel the inside of his girl and eat her pussy until she cried.

Once the towels were discarded, Mateo climbed back in bed and tried to steady his spinning head. Lux cuddled up to him, glad to have him back, before she quickly fell asleep. Mateo passed out from the liquor he consumed not too long after.

The next morning, Mateo woke up in a great mood, despite being a bit hungover. He spent the greater part of the day yesterday drinking, and the shit was definitely catching up with him today. It was all good, though. He looked to the side of him and saw Lux sleeping peacefully. She was truly a work of art. He trailed a finger down her curvy body, admiring her mocha colored skin that was so soft. As a light sleeper, Lux's eyes fluttered open, and Mateo smiled.

"Good morning," he said before leaning down and kissing her full lips.

Lux groaned and stretched and then smiled. "Good morning, papi. What time is it?"

Mateo grabbed his phone off the nightstand and looked at the time. "Just after nine."

"Damn," Lux groaned. "I have to meet up with Blanca at ten to get her dress fitted."

Mateo threw the covers off his naked body and got out of bed. He stretched before swaggering over to the balcony door and windows and sliding the blackout curtains open. The sun shined through, causing Lux to squint her eyes. Mateo loved the brightness. He looked out at the ocean and took a deep breath, thankful that today seemed to be the first step to getting things back on track and normal. He turned to face Lux, whose eyes immediately dropped to his stiff dick. Mateo smirked as he walked back over to her. "You know, you can kiss it if you want."

Lux gulped. She did want to, but she remained strong. At this point, she looked at it as get-back at him for not bending to allow her to push the wedding back. She got up on her knees and crawled over to his side of the bed before putting her arms around his neck, his dick poking her in her belly button. Mateo grabbed a handful of her juicy ass and moaned slightly, loving the feel of her. Lux smiled in his face and said, "Not a chance, papi. You can wait a few more weeks."

Mateo chuckled and slapped her ass. Lux bit her lip, liking the sting.

"As long as it's a few more weeks and not a few more months," Mateo replied before kissing her cheek and walking into the bathroom. He had a full day of meetings with some connects through some of the surrounding islands, so he shouted over his shoulder, "I'll be home late, but let's have dinner tonight, eh?"

Lux crawled out of bed and stretched again before walking over to him. "It's a date, but how about I join you in the shower? I need to get ready quickly so I'm not late meeting up with B."

Mateo groaned. "Chaparrita… you're not making this waiting shit easy on me."

Lux smirked and walked past him before throwing over her shoulder, "It's just a shower, Papi."

Mateo watched as her ass jiggled with every step, and he looked down at his stiff dick and shook his head. "Fine, but make it a cold shower."

Lux giggled and turned on the rainfall shower before beckoning him to join as she stepped under the stream of water. Mateo bit his lip and followed his future wife's commands with a smile on his face.

CHAPTER

Lux finished getting dressed in a fitted Burberry dress with the matching tennis shoes before making her way down the stairs. Mateo rushed out the door about half an hour ago after a steamy make-out session in the shower. She texted Blanca ten minutes ago letting her know she would be a few minutes late, to which Blanca finally replied, *figured.*

Lux smirked at her phone as she made her way into the kitchen. She was notorious for being late if it wasn't about some money, and everyone who loved her knew it.

"What are you smiling at?" Dionne asked as she placed a plate of food in front of Waylan, who was sitting at the island counter.

"Blanca," Lux replied before kissing her father on the cheek and sitting next to him. "Mama, can you cut me up a mango like you used to do?"

Dionne smiled. "Anything for you, baby."

Lux wanted to get something on her stomach before she left, because knowing Blanca, she was going to have her at that dress shop all damn day, even though both their dresses were already picked out. She had a thing about trying on wedding dresses, even though she didn't even have a man, and Lux thought it was cute. She honestly couldn't wait until the day Blanca got everything her heart desired. A good man and the wedding of her dreams. As scary as getting married was for Lux, she had to admit the anticipation felt great and caused butterflies and shit in her stomach.

"What are you up to today, nena? Want to hit the shooting range?" Waylan asked as he ate his eggs and chorizo. Lux knew he was referring to the range they had in their basement because any other range wouldn't do with how crazy they got sometimes. Nah, they needed to be insane with their weapons in private. Otherwise, people would be looking at them like they were… well… insane. They wouldn't really be wrong, either.

Lux nudged her father with a smirk. "Can't, Papa. Blanca and I are going to get her dress fitted today."

He nodded. "I suppose you'll be trying on dresses all afternoon?"

Dionne giggled. When Lux first showed an interest in dress shopping as an adult, Dionne took her and Blanca to her favorite stores, and Blanca was into it more than the three of them combined. By the time the day was finished, Dionne was exhausted and vowed to never step foot in a bridal store with Blanca again. She loved the girl, but she didn't want to watch her try on every bridesmaid and wedding dress known to man.

"You already know," Lux replied just as her mother sat a bowl of cut fresh mango in front of her. It was topped with honey and Tajin, just the way Lux liked it.

She ate quickly, listening to her parent's idle chatter. When she finished, she hastily washed the bowl out and set it on the drying rack before texting Blanca that she was on her way.

"I'll see you later," Lux called over her shoulder on her way out the door.

"Wait!" Dionne called.

Lux stopped in her tracks and turned to her mother. "Qué pasa?"

"I was thinking of doing family dinner tonight. Why don't you invite Blanca and Dalia?"

Lux shook her head. "I wish I could, Mama, but Mateo wants to do dinner tonight, just me and him."

Dionne's eyebrows rose while Waylan looked on in interest. "Did he come back? I haven't seen him. You two must have talked?"

Lux realized that in her rush this morning she forgot to mention to her parents that she and Mateo were back on track. She grinned as she looked at her father. "You'll be happy to know that the wedding is on for the original date."

A smile broke across his face, and he stood with his arms out so he could hug his baby girl. "I'm glad to hear that."

He kissed the top of her head while her mother looked on with a soft smile on her face, but Lux didn't miss the worry in her eyes. Before she could assure Dionne that everything was okay, Dionne spoke. "You're sure about this?"

"Yes, Mama. I am. I want to marry Mateo, so there is no need to put the wedding off. I'm actually getting kind of excited. Between him and Blanca, their excitement is rubbing off on me. It's starting to feel like I'm a little girl again, dreaming up my wedding. But now, it's reality. I'll be married in just a few short weeks!"

Dionne's face broke out into a genuine smile. She was relieved that Lux seemed to be sure about her decision, and more importantly, excited. No bride should dread her wedding day, and that was Dionne's biggest fear in this entire situation as she was growing up. Arranged marriages were tricky, and she had been determined to make sure her daughter had some of the normal experiences children should have growing up. Even though it was arranged, Dionne wanted the wedding to be as normal as possible for her daughter, and she was glad there was a genuine love between Lux and Mateo.

"Alright, baby," Dionne conceded.

Lux smiled at her parents one last time before waving and saying, "I'll see you two later. Te amo."

She rushed through the house and out the front door. Once she was safely tucked inside her car, she cranked it up and peeled out of the driveway and through the security gate that held no security. Her family didn't need that shit. It was an unspoken rule not to fuck with the Rose family. Nobody quite knew why. They just gave off the vibe that if anyone tried them, they would be sorry for it.

Ten minutes later, Lux was pulling into the bridal shop parking lot after blasting Cardi B the entire way. She loved her some Cardi, and any time she was alone in a car, she had her own variation of a Bardi concert. She parked and grabbed her purse before rushing into the store. The cool air hit her as soon as she stepped into the small boutique, and she was immediately greeted by a sales lady, Maria.

"Ms. Rose, you made it." She beamed.

Lux looked down at the Christian Dior watch that graced her dainty wrist, noting that she was only fifteen minutes late, but late, none the less. "Yeah, sorry about that. My mama always says I'm going to be late for my own funeral."

Maria giggled before leading her toward the back of the shop where Blanca came into view. Lux smirked. Her best friend was standing in front of the wall to ceiling mirror admiring the white dress she had on.

"Started early, eh?" Lux asked.

Blanca looked at her in the mirror with a grin stretched across her face. "You were late, so I took the opportunity to try a few dresses on. Maria showed me some new ones."

Maria smiled. "Isn't it gorgeous on her?"

Lux nodded. It was. The dress hugged Blanca's slim figure and lifted her small breasts, making them look bigger than normal. It was a sensual gown with a long train. "I don't know, B. We might have to put that one on hold for you for when you get married. It's the prettiest one I've ever seen you try on."

Blanca whirled around and beamed at her friend. "You think so?"

Lux nodded, and then Blanca's face fell. Lux's brows furrowed. "What's wrong, chica?"

Blanca looked down at her feet and said, "I'll never be able to afford a gown like this."

Lux knew Blanca had it hard. She worked was a manager at a hotel, but the job didn't pay a whole lot. She still lived with Dalia, even though she could afford a nice one bedroom apartment on her own. Blanca didn't want to leave her aunt alone, and she helped her aunt out financially, too. She was getting older, and even though Dalia insisted Blanca go on and live her life, Blanca refused. She felt she owed Dalia for taking her in and caring for her all those years.

Lux walked up to Blanca and hugged her. "Ah, B. Don't you even worry about that because you're going to marry a rich ass chulo who will give you your hearts desires, and if he doesn't, you know damn well Mat and I will make sure your wedding is exactly what you want it to be."

Blanca's eyes lit up, and she spun around again to look at herself in the mirror, running her hand down the soft fabric of the dress as her head tilted to the side, causing her sleek black hair to fall to one side. "Do you really think I'll get married one day, Lux?"

"I know you will," Lux replied with a genuine smile. "If anyone deserves a fairytale wedding, it's you."

Blanca nodded once in the mirror and turned to Maria. "I guess it's time to take this off. We have Lux's wedding to focus on. I'm ready to try on my bridesmaid's dress!"

Maria nodded and helped Blanca down from the podium she had been standing on, and the two disappeared behind a curtain in the corner. After a moment, Maria emerged, and Lux motioned her over.

"Maria, put that dress on my account. I'll come back and get it another time," Lux whispered. When the time was right, Lux would surprise her best friend with the wedding dress of her dreams, and she truly could not wait for that day to come.

Maria's smile was a mile wide as unshed tears graced her eyes. "Oh, Ms. Rose... you're such a good friend."

The older woman patted Lux's hand before disappearing to the front of the store to do as she was told.

After a few more minutes, Blanca re-emerged from behind the curtain, and Lux's heart leaped. There was something about seeing her best friend in her bridesmaid dress that made the entire thing real for her. Blanca smiled and stepped onto the podium, looking at herself in the mirror. Like the other dress, this one hugged Blanca's small frame, but the dress was a coral color that popped against her pale skin. The dress had a small train, and there was a plunging neckline that showed off her small chest. The shit was sexy as hell. As the only bridesmaid in the wedding, Lux wanted Blanca to shine that day.

"B, that dress is sexy as fuck. Let me find out you're going to outshine me on my day," Lux joked.

Blanca smiled. "It is sexy, huh? Maybe I'll catch they eye of a man and find my husband."

Lux giggled. "I don't know if there is anyone our age that will be there that you don't already know."

Blanca shrugged. "We'll see."

Maria came back and grinned at Blanca. "This dress was made for you, chica."

Blanca nodded, and Maria got to work pinning the dress in places that needed to be taken in. When she got to the bottom of the dress, she asked, "Do you know what shoes you will be wearing for the wedding?"

Blanca nodded and looked at Lux. "Can you grab them out of my bag?"

Lux looked to where her friend was pointing and spotted the golden heels they picked out months ago sticking out from an oversized purse sitting in a plush chair. She grabbed them and noticed Blanca's phone was ringing inside the purse. The caller ID said *bae,* and a grin stretched across Lux's face. She grabbed the phone as well and presented the shoes to her friend before flashing the phone at her. "And who might bae be?"

Blanca's eyes widened, and she tried snatching the phone from Lux. "Lux, stop playing."

"Oh, you don't want me to answer and grill him, eh?" Lux teased.

"No!" Blanca shouted as she reached for the phone again, nearly knocking Maria over.

Lux chuckled and tossed Blanca the phone. She caught it effortlessly and visibly relaxed. "Chill, chica. I won't be nosy today. Just know I expect to meet him soon. Looks like you don't need to catch the eye of another man. Why not bring your *bae* to the wedding instead?"

Blanca thought about it and said, "I don't even know if we will be seeing each other by the end of the year."

Lux grinned. "Good thing the wedding is going to be in a few weeks then."

Blanca's eyes ballooned, and she broke out into a huge smile. "Swear?"

"Swear." Lux giggled.

Blanca shimmied and looked down at Maria, who was trying to get Blanca to step into the heels. Once she did, she said, "Looks like we will need this dress back pronto, Maria. We have a wedding to attend!"

Maria shrugged since she didn't know the wedding date had been in danger of being pushed back, and Lux giggled.

Ten minutes later, Blanca was back in her regular clothes, and Maria looked at Lux and asked, "Do you want to try your dress on, Ms. Rose? I completed the alterations. I know you have a final fitting in a couple of weeks, but we could try it on now, too, if you want."

Lux thought about it and shrugged her shoulders. "Why not?"

She figured putting the dress on might further grow her excitement, and what woman didn't like trying on her wedding dress any chance she got?

Maria beamed and scurried off to grab Lux's dress. When she returned, the two went into the dressing room, and Lux undressed so she was completely naked. No panties or bra could be worn with this tight ass dress. Maria helped her maneuver into it, and when they finally emerged, Lux had a huge smile on her face, but Blanca had her face buried in her phone.

"Ahem," Lux said, dramatically clearing her throat.

Blanca looked up and smiled at her friend. "Lux, you look beautiful!"

Lux beamed and stepped up onto the podium so she could see herself.

"Let me grab your veil," Maria said before disappearing again.

Lux ran her hand down the diamond studded bodice. Her chest was huge in the dress, but it looked the fuck good. Like Blanca's dress, there was a plunging neckline, and her big titties sat up just right, showing off an ample amount of cleavage that was sure to drive Mateo wild. The mesh lace on the neckline made it more classy, and the diamonds covering the dress in an intricate pattern made her literally shine. Her flat stomach gave way to her wide hips. The dress fit her ass tightly and bunched up in the back, giving way to a long train.

When Maria came back into view and placed the diamond tiara with the veil attached on Lux's head, tears formed in her eyes. She pictured Mateo seeing her in this dress for the first time, and her heart rate sped up. She glanced at Blanca, who was still focused on her phone. Lux didn't mind, though. This moment was a bit personal. It was the moment she finally felt ready for the future that had been planned out for her from birth.

"I'm really going to be Ms. Rodriguez," Lux whispered.

Blanca looked up at her friend and placed a smile on her face, but Lux didn't even notice as she gazed at herself in the mirror.

CHAPTER

"**P**api, this is so nice," Lux gushed as she looked around at the scenery.

Mateo rented a beach house not far from her parents' home for the evening. Even though there wouldn't be any fucking involved, Mateo wanted to get his girl alone. It was something he made sure to do frequently in their adult life, and Lux always appreciated it.

Tonight, he had a chef set up a beach dinner at sunset, and Lux was so at peace. She absolutely loved the water, so any time she was close to it, she felt at ease. Mateo knew this, which was why he had the night set up by the ocean and with her favorite foods, although, she wasn't paying much attention to the spread in front of them. Her focus was on the water.

Mateo grabbed Lux's dainty manicured hand and caressed it. "I'm glad you like it, chaparrita. You know I would do anything for you."

Lux turned to him with a radiant smile. "I know, Mateo."

He noticed her blush and gave her a small grin. "I appreciate you the past couple of weeks, mami. You really been holding me down since my parents died."

He cleared his throat, and Lux could see he was trying to hide his emotion. "You don't have to do that."

"Do what?" he asked, genuinely confused.

"Hide your feelings from me. I know you miss them. It's weird for me, too. They've been around me since I was a baby," Lux replied honestly. She may not have had a loving relationship with his parents, but she did care about them. Their absence was definitely felt.

Mateo chuckled to lighten the mood. "Says the woman who never cries."

Lux shrugged. "I'm just saying. This is a safe place."

Mateo gave her a charming smile. "I know, mami. You are my safe place. I love you. I know I hurt your feelings when we had our disagreement the other day, but I felt like I was losing everything, you know? My parents… you… I felt crazy. Thank you for being the bigger person and willing to compromise. I know you have your reservations, but I'll make sure our day is perfect."

"I tried on my dress today." Lux beamed. "And I finally realized that in a few weeks I'll be married to my best friend. I felt silly for even suggesting we push the wedding back, Mateo. I apologize."

Mateo lifted her hand to his mouth and kissed it. "Don't apologize, baby. It's all in the past, and once we are married, we can take our family businesses to the next level. We can leave a legacy for our own children."

Lux's smile faltered. She was never sure about wanting children of her own. While Blanca couldn't wait to be a mommy, Lux was a bit more apprehensive. She wasn't sure if she had a motherly instinct, but Mateo had always been so pressed about having children that she never spoke on it. She figured if it happened, she would deal with it.

The mention of their family businesses made her squirm in her seat as well. She still wasn't sure how he would take her true occupation, but it was something she couldn't worry herself with. She knew Mateo loved her, and they would get past that little speed bump when the time came, so she redirected the conversation. "Speaking of your family business. Have you figured all that out? I know it's been stressful for you keeping things afloat."

Mateo nodded. "It has, but luckily, a few of my father's workers have been helpful in keeping things running smooth. Oh, and I forgot to tell you, the insurance policy paid out. That shit is going right into the kids' college funds."

Mateo's lopsided grin made her smile, despite the nervous butterflies going rampant in her stomach. Maybe it was conversations like these that made her want to push the wedding back in the first place… so she could work up the courage to tell Mateo how she really felt. If only he knew that she was an assassin… maybe he would understand that she had a certain lifestyle to maintain. She wasn't sure kids fit into that.

She shifted in her seat and said, "I'm glad things are settling down, Mat. I hope over the next few weeks leading up to the wedding you can relax a little more."

Mateo smiled at her guiltily. Part of the reason he asked her out to this lavish private dinner in the first place was because of what he was about to say next. "Actually, mami… I been meaning to tell you that I have to go out of town for a few days."

Lux's thick brows arched together as she pulled her hand away from him. "When, Mat? We are getting married in three weeks. There's so much shit that needs to be done. I need you here."

He grabbed at the back of his neck, knowing she wasn't going to like what he had to say. "Tonight—"

"Mateo!" Lux screeched. "For how long, papi?"

Her lips pulled together in a pout, and Mateo tried not to smile because she honestly looked so cute. "A few days, Lux, but I promise—"

"Mateo, your parents just died. You're about to get married in a few weeks. You need a break to regroup and focus on our day. Can't this wait?"

Lux was starting to feel like she should have stuck with her gut and pushed the wedding back. It didn't seem like Mateo's head was really where she needed it to be.

What Mateo didn't understand was that Lux needed him. That completely went over his head because she had a hard time asking people for anything, but she desperately needed her fiancé to be present with her over the next few weeks so she could feel better about this entire thing. She was an overthinker, and Mateo could calm her nerves just by being present.

"It can't wait, mami. I promise I'll be back before you know it, and then I'll be all in. You just make sure you don't get any mysterious work calls on our wedding day," Mateo replied seriously.

Lux couldn't help the giggle that escaped her pouty lips. She and her father already decided that whatever jobs came through, he would come out of retirement and take them on for her while she prepared for the wedding. Lux grabbed his hand again and sighed. "Daddy is taking over for me until after the honeymoon. Just… get back here quickly, okay?"

Mateo nodded, happy that she didn't throw a complete fit. Lux was good for doing that shit if she didn't get her way. She didn't throw tantrums, she would just cuss a mothafucka clean the fuck out until they bent to her will. An alpha female to the fullest. Luckily, he caught her on a good day or some shit because she saved that, and he was forever grateful for that small miracle.

"You got it, mami."

Lux sighed. "Does that mean we don't get to enjoy this beautiful house?"

She gestured toward the beach house behind him, and he looked at her guiltily. "I was hoping you would enjoy it for the both of us. I had the staff run you a hot bath before they left, and they left out desserts and shit."

Mateo knew better than to keep the staff around. Lux's family was weird about that shit for some reason. They couldn't fully relax until they were left with only the people they trusted. That meant no staff or anyone to make their lives easier. Mateo always found it strange because he grew up on staff being around the house.

Lux opened her mouth to respond, but Mateo's phone ringing interrupted her. He glanced at it and silenced it before looking back at her. "I want you to enjoy yourself tonight, okay? And relax."

Lux nodded sadly and asked, "Will you at least be able to finish dinner and maybe have some dessert with me?"

Mateo was about to respond when his phone rang again. Lux's brows rose as she watched him silence his phone again. He looked up at her and said, "Work."

A series of texts came through before Lux could reply. "Do you need to get that?"

He shook his head before standing to his feet. He reached his arms out for her, and Lux reluctantly allowed him to pull her into his arms, not liking where this was headed.

"They need me to come handle some shit right now, Lux. I'm sorry," he said solemnly.

Lux let out a deep breath and nodded her head. "Go ahead. Thanks for dinner."

Mateo tilted her head and kissed her lips. "Anything for you, mi amor."

He pulled away, and she looked up at him. "Maybe I'll call Blanca to come over. Have a girl's night."

He stuffed his phone in his pocket and looked at her sadly. "I talked to her earlier, and she said she was working a double at the hotel."

"Damn," Lux whispered. She had half a mind to just go back to her parents. She didn't mind being alone, but she had been looking forward to a romantic evening with her fiancé, so she was a bit disappointed, but she realized this was what came with the territory of being in a relationship with a drug dealer. She knew there were times she had to pick up and leave because she got a job, so she realized she needed to give her soon to be husband some grace. She stood on her tiptoes and kissed his lips once more before saying, "Go, papi. Come back to me safely."

He smiled down at her and kissed her nose before walking past her and calling over his shoulder, "I'll call when I can."

Lux waved at his back and sat back down in her chair, looking at the delicious meal and then at the ocean. She decided she was going to stuff her face, go back into the house, change into the swimsuit Mateo told her to pack, and then go for a swim. She realized only the ocean could instantly cheer her up just like that as she grabbed for a crab leg and cracked it open like a pro, patiently counting down the minutes until Mateo came back so they could enjoy the countdown to their quickly approaching wedding.

CHAPTER

Mateo rushed through the home he rented for Lux and dashed through the front door. Once he was in his truck, he pulled his phone out of his pocket. It rang before he could even unlock his screen. He sighed heavily before answering it. "Yo, what's up? I was in the middle of something."

"Meet me at the spot," the voice on the other end responded.

"We weren't supposed to meet until later. You had me rushing out of dinner—"

"See you in a few."

The line disconnected, and Mateo blew out a frustrated breath before starting his car and pulling out of the driveway.

He drove the entire fifteen minutes in silence, contemplating how he even got himself into this predicament. When he arrived at his location, he parked in the parking lot and made his way into the lobby. He bypassed the front desk and headed straight for the elevators. Once he was inside and pressed the top floor, he took his wallet out of his pocket and produced a room key. It was a room key he always had on hand because he paid for this room for an entire year. The year mark was actually coming up, so he would be handing the key in soon, but that was something he didn't even want to think about. The day he handed that room key in meant he no longer needed the room. No longer needing the room was an entire onslaught of new issues he would have to face.

When Lux asked him to push the wedding off, he was a bit relieved at first, which was why he didn't put up much of a fuss. He actually considered her proposition. Pushing the wedding back would give him time to think, but when his mistress found out about it, she damn near beat his ass. She wanted this wedding to happen more than anyone, which seemed strange, right? Not in this situation. In this little love triangle, the motivation was money. Greed was the only thing that caused this tangled web, and before Mateo knew it, he was caught up without a fuckin' backbone or say in any of the shit.

He made it to the executive room and opened the door, slipping inside before anyone could see him.

He spotted her on the bed in a red bra and panties set. His dick instantly got hard, which pissed him off even further because that shit was exactly what got him in this situation in the first place.

"Why did you need me to rush here so early, B?"

Blanca Perez stood from the bed and sashayed over to Mateo, placing a hand on his chest and forming a pout on her face. "I missed you, papi."

Mateo scoffed. "Blanca, you're off the chain, man. I was with Lux. She could have seen it was you blowing me up."

Blanca rolled her eyes. "I told you to change my name in your phone, estúpido. Thank God I did. When you called me earlier, I was with her, and she almost answered. Would have blown this entire thing."

Mateo's eyes widened. "Man, nah… B, we need to chill on this shit, for real. I can't—"

Blanca slapped him lightly on the cheek as she looked up into his eyes. Her ass had a spell on him since they were young, and Lux was too blinded by love and the fairytale land her parents created for her to even notice.

Mateo looked down at the woman who had single-handedly fucked his happily ever after up back when they were young teens. She was the reason he stayed up at night while guilt consumed him. She was the reason he lashed out at Lux sometimes. She was the reason he couldn't answer for Lux for hours on end. Sometimes days. He wasn't working. He had workers for that. All he had to do was sit back and collect money. That was how his father set his operation up, but Lux didn't know that. She was out there chasing a bag and working hard, and she assumed her man was doing the same. Truth be told, Mateo had never worked a day in his life. Money came to him, and that was all he needed to know.

Nah, he was out her fucking. Him and Blanca used to fuck wherever and whenever they could. They once did it at Lux's home, even. Once Blanca got the job at the hotel, this became their rendezvous spot. He could never bring her home because his parents would have his head for fucking up the contract they had in place to marry Lux. They stood to gain a lot once the marriage was finalized. It was too bad they died before they could get whatever it was they wanted out of the deal. Unfortunately for him, Blanca wanted this wedding to happen. She had a plan, and Mateo was spellbound by the pussy to go through with it. He was a puppet, and she was the puppeteer. Whatever she wanted, she got… and what she wanted more than anything was Lux's life.

"You can, and you will," Blanca replied coolly. "Don't worry, once the ink dries and you're entitled to everything the Rose family has, we can kill Lux so you can rest easy at night. Then… you and I can get married. That's the plan, right?"

Blanca was wrong. Killing Lux would not put his mind at ease. Despite how shitty he had been to her behind her back, he really did love Lux. He just loved the pussy Blanca was giving him more. It was unfortunate, but it was real life shit.

"We could have just broke off the engagement with her and eloped, B. We don't have to do her like this. I have more than enough money for us, especially since I got the insurance policy—"

Blanca cut him off again with a scoff. "Your money is great, papi, but you know the goal. Think of all we can do with the Rose family's money and yours? We would be at the top of the world, baby. And when the dust settles, I can give you a couple of babies, and we can live the life we fucking deserve… finally. Just us, far away from here, papi. It's always been our dream."

Mateo nodded, although he didn't fully agree. His dream had always been split between Blanca and Lux. If only he could mesh the two of them together, he would be the happiest man on the planet, but that wasn't possible, and Blanca had been becoming more reckless the closer they got to the wedding. He was at his wit's end and didn't know which way to turn.

Blanca smiled up at him, oblivious to his inner turmoil. Either that or she really didn't give a fuck. She grew up in Lux's shadow, always receiving her hand-me-downs and having to compete with her lavish lifestyle. A bitch was tired as fuck, but the end was near. Her future would really be able to start once the wedding was finished and Mateo could take the bitch for everything she owned. Once he had her bank accounts and assets secured, Blanca could swoop in and put a bullet through her best friend's skull. She dreamed about that shit. It got her off on nights when Mateo was with Lux.

Now, Lux's parents could get a bit of mercy. She would let them keep their house and maybe even throw them a chunk of change since they had been so good to her all these years, but they would damn sure be spending the rest of their lives grieving for their precious daughter.

An evil glint sparkled in Blanca's eyes as she went over the plan in her head before she dropped to her knees and unbuckled Mateo's belt. He watched, half in guilt and the other half in lust as she pulled his dick out of his pants.

Blanca looked up at him with a devilish grin before she slipped her hand in her panties, playing in her wetness. "It's almost time, Mateo. Soon, we will be rid of Lux Rose, but we will gain all her fuckin' money. You ready, papi?"

She didn't give him time to respond as she swallowed his dick whole. Mateo forgot the question within seconds as he palmed the back of Blanca's head and enjoyed the sensation. She was the only woman that had ever made him feel this way. Not even Lux could tap into his sexual side just yet because she was holding out, but Blanca? She had been giving it up since they were thirteen years old, and she had long since become a pro. She mastered his body and knew how to make him bend to her will.

Mateo watched her and forgot all about Lux for the time being, which was unfortunate. Neither one of them truly knew who they were dealing with. They'd better both pray their plan went off without a glitch because if Lux caught wind of what they were up to… red would douse the city.

To be continued…

Please don't forget to leave a review! They mean so much to me, and they help more than you think! Don't have time to leave a review? Give it a rating - it takes 2 seconds!

AUTHR NOTE

Whew! Y'all… what do you think is going to
happen?
I want you to remember, this book is just the
beginning of Lux's story. Next, you will get the
middle, and finally, the end. This book was strictly
for backstory and build up - but don't worry! Part 2
is coming way sooner than you think!
I can't want for you all to see what happens next with
Lux, Mateo, and Blanca…

Stay tuned!
 Cyn

Up Next...

CYN'S CATALOG

Get signed copies at: Cynful Monarch

Dust 2 Diamonds

The Baddest of Them All

Lil Red Ryder

Rebel & Her Beast

A Fairytale Wedding

The Princess & the Goon

The Urban Fairytale Series Complete Collection

Baby, it's Cold Outside

Bosses Link Up

Billion Dollar Baddie

Billion Dollar Baddie 2

A Hood Chick's Savior

Anything for the Family

Anything for the Family 2

Endlessly Mine

Hell Hath No Fury: Beaten at Your Own Game

The Married Woman

LET'S CONNECT!

Join my readers group on Facebook, and stay up on all releases, get character visuals and sneak peeks, and even get in on giveaways!
https://www.facebook.com/groups/277463019954112/

Sign up for my email list! Get exclusive content and discounts!
https://bit.ly/39tvXOC

WHILE YOU'RE WAITING...
READ THIS BOOK BY CYN... NOW AVAILABLE!

HELL HATH NO FURY: BEATEN AT YOUR OWN GAME
Chapter 4 Sneak Peek

Running late was not something I liked doing, especially when the person I was meeting was my best friend. Maryana would surely have several words to exchange with me when I finally made it to the restaurant, but I had one piece of business to take care of before I could spend the afternoon catching up with her before my next patient.

I was annoyed with myself that I'd forgotten the check for the contractors for the clinic once again. She called me this morning and reminded me I needed to make that payment or they would stop work until it was paid. I assured Bryson I had the financial shit covered, so I knew I needed to handle this before I did anything else. I couldn't let him down. This was too much of a big deal to do that to him, and I'd put too much money into this shit to slow the process up over a forgotten check.

I put pressure on the gas pedal as I sped toward my house so I could get to Maryana quicker. My stomach rumbling only reinforced my rushing, and before I knew it, I was pulling up to my home. I was surprised to see Bryson's car in the circular drive-way. I figured he would be at the construction site where he was every damn day, overseeing the building process and making sure everything was perfect. He was a perfectionist in that way, but I loved that about him because so was I. It was the reason we lived together so well right off the bat. Everything was in its place, and we never had to argue about the house being too messy or one of us not cleaning up after ourselves. It truly was the perfect union once we got over the hurdle of the financial differences.

I left my car running and got out quickly, knowing I would be in and out. My checkbook was in my home office, and the check was already written out laying right on top of it, which was why I could have kicked myself for forgetting it this morning because I walked right past it to grab my laptop.

I rushed inside and headed straight for the stairs, only briefly wondering where Bryson was. I was on a mission, and I figured I would ask him why he was home this afternoon later on. I rushed down the hall and into my office just as my phone vibrated in my pocket. I pulled it out and glanced at the caller ID, seeing that it was Maryana.

"Shit," I cursed under my breath, deciding to ignore the call and text her once I was back in the car and on the way. It was better to let her know I was en route than telling her I made a detour all the way home, which was why I was running late.

I grabbed the check and then hustled out of the room, closing my office door behind me. As I bustled past our bedroom, I heard slow music playing, and I slowed for a moment, cocking my head to the side and wondering why our Alexa speaker was on. I figured Bryson was in there chillin', but that was so odd for him to do in the middle of a workday. I knew he had practice later on, and normally, he would fill his mornings with working on shit for the clinic. I briefly wondered if he was sick before I decided to do an about-face and check in on him quickly.

I eased the door open quietly in case he was sleeping. If he was, I wasn't going to bother waking him because I really had to get going, anyway, but Bryson was definitely not sleeping. In fact, he was wide awake and pummeling his dick into some random bitch... in our bed. I stared at them for a moment in confusion. I was fully convinced that what I was seeing was a dream. I knew there was no way in hell my husband was fucking another bitch, who had the fucking audacity to be pretty as hell, I might add, in our bed. In *my* home. This shit was mine. Bryson never wanted parts of this house, so he agreed to move in but he never wanted to be added to the deed. I didn't push him on that... and now, I idly wondered if that was a good thing. Maybe that was divine intervention because the scene before me had me thinking about all the dirty shit I wanted to do to him. Kicking him out, for starters. I reared back at that thought and closed the door quietly before turning around and walking back through the house in a daze.

Could I really kick my husband out? Hell yeah, I could after what I just saw, but he was my husband. It was like my brain wasn't computing the shit I just witnessed. I felt like I had completely shut down. For as smart as I was, this shit had me stuck on stupid.

I walked out the front door and closed it before locking up in a daze. When I finally got back in my car, I started it and pulled out of the driveway, mindlessly driving toward the restaurant Maryana was waiting for me at. I was on autopilot as I tried piecing together what was happening in my life. I felt numb. The shit just wasn't processing.

Before I knew it, I was sitting in the parking lot of the restaurant. I grabbed my purse and got out of the car, still in a daze. When I walked into the restaurant, I spotted Maryana right away. She was sitting at a table looking down at her phone, no doubt pissed at me. I ignored the hostess speaking to me. I wasn't even sure what she said. I bypassed her and headed straight for Maryana, tears building up in my eyes the closer I got. When I plopped down in the seat across from her, she looked up, startled.

"About time, bi... Nia, what's wrong?"

My eyes slowly moved up to her face, and I saw concern written all over her face. a tear finally fell from my left eye as I said, "I just caught Bryson cheating on me."

Maryana blinked at me as I stared at her. I was hoping she could shed some light on this shit because I was having a hard time figuring it out by myself. Her blue eyes bore into mine, and I could see the same confusion she possessed was the same confusion within me. I sighed heavily before slouching back in my chair.

The waitress came by the table and asked me something, but I didn't hear her, nor did I care. I wasn't trying to be rude... I literally just couldn't right now. Thankfully, Maryana responded to her, and she finally walked away before my best friend grabbed my hand, pulling my attention back to her.

"Nia, what happened? What do you mean Bryson is cheating on you?"

I knew I just said the words out loud myself, but hearing them was an entirely different concept. I cocked my head at her, and the confusion only grew stronger. Those words strung together in the same sentence in exactly that order wasn't computing for me at all.

"He was having sex," I said slowly while looking into her eyes. "But not with me."

Maryana's confusion turned into rage. She was like that. Going from zero to one thousand in the blink of an eye. I wished I possessed that quality at this moment. Anything would be better than the utter confusion and numbness.

"Did you kill them both? I hope the fuck you did! Where were you, Nia? Where is he now? Wait until I tell Jamel about this-"

"I didn't do anything," I said blankly.

"Honey, I know you didn't do anything to deserve thi-" Maryana looked at me with sympathy in her eyes, but I shook my head vigorously, and she stopped talking mid-sentence.

"No, Maryana. I mean, I didn't do anything when I saw them. I simply closed the door and walked out of the house-"

"Hold up," Maryana growled as she put her hand up. "You mean to tell me that bum ass bitch had another hoe in your house?"

"In my bed," I confirmed.

"Oh, hell no. We are going over there right the fuck now, Nia. Do you hear me?" Maryana stood to her feet and started gathering her things, but I stopped her.

"No."

She stopped what she was doing and looked at me like I had just asked her to square dance. "No?"

I nodded. "I'm not going back over there."

"That is your mothafucking house, Nia!" Maryana shouted, and I winced.

"I know, Maryana," I hissed. "I will go back there when I'm ready, but I just can't right now. I can't."

My voice cracked on the last word, and tears flooded my eyes and spilled over. I put my face in my hands and sobs wracked through my body as it dawned on what Bryson had done. He completely flipped my life upside down in seconds. I had no idea what I was going to do from here, but I knew I needed to stay away from him and get my head on straight so I could figure out my next move. Going back to my house and fucking Bryson and his bitch up wasn't the answer, as much as I wanted to do just that the more I thought about it.

Maryana came around the table and wrapped her arms around me as I cried, consoling me and whispering affirmations into my ear.

When I finally calmed down, she pulled back and said, "Whatever you need, I'm here for you. You are not alone, Nia. I have your back whatever you want to do, but you can't pretend like nothing happened, boo. You will need to face Bryson one way or another."

I knew she was right, and I welcomed that thought, but the shit would be on my time. I nodded and said, "I'm going to deal with him. Best believe that, Maryana."

She must have seen the glint in my puffy red eyes because the corner of her mouth turned up in a lopsided grin. "What do you have up your sleeve, sis? I'm down for some get-back."

I shook my head. "I'm not really sure yet, but I do know it starts with this."

I pulled my purse into my lap from where I discarded it on the floor and then I grasped the check that had caused me to find out Bryson's dirty little secret. Without thinking about it, I tore the check up and knew I would never write another one. Fuck him and that clinic. Tomorrow, I would call the contractors and get as much money back from the project as I possibly could. Any money I lost I would charge to the game. Whether Bryson and I could work through this shit... I wasn't sure, but I was one hundred percent certain that bad dogs didn't get treats, so unless he found someone else to fund his clinic, he could kiss that shit goodbye.

Hey There!

Thank you for your support on my literary journey. I hope your reading experience was a pleasant one. Please leave a review on Goodreads and Amazon. Please feel free to connect with me to stay current on upcoming releases and reader specific exclusives.